RACE TO REVENGE

ART OF PAYBACK
BOOK 1

DAN PETROSINI

Joe,
You never really
know someone!

DAN PETROSINI
MYSTERY & SUSPENSE AUTHOR
www.danpetrosini.com

Print ISBN: 978-1-960286-26-0
Kindle ISBN: 978-1-960286-25-3
Printed in Naples, FL
Library of Congress Control Number: Pending

The Luca Mystery Series

Am I the Killer

Vanished

The Serenity Murder

Third Chances

A Cold, Hard Case

Cop or Killer?

Silencing Salter

A Killer Missteps

Uncertain Stakes

The Grandpa Killer

Dangerous Revenge

Where Are They

Buried at the Lake

The Preserve Killer

No One is Safe

Murder, Money and Mayhem

Suspenseful Secrets

Cory's Dilemma

Cory's Flight

Cory's Shift

Art Of Payback

Race To Revenge

Other works by Dan Petrosini

The Final Enemy

Complicit Witness

Push Back

Ambition Cliff

ACKNOWLEDGMENTS

I'm grateful for the love and support of my wife, Julie, and our daughters, Stephanie and Jennifer.

A special thanks to Scott Klabunde, whose quiet passion for exotic cars provided the inspiration to dip a toe into that world.

PROLOGUE

THINGS WERE BETTER SINCE WE ESCAPED FROM FOSTER CARE. But there was unfinished business. The day to even the score had finally arrived.

The moon was shrouded in clouds. Mario parked the car four blocks away from the water, on the northern edge of Sea Girt, New Jersey. It was perfect; January ensured the area was desolate.

As Mario cut the engine, my stomach dropped. Could I do it? I stuck my fingers under my hat, fingering the scar that had shifted my life as much as Mom getting murdered.

It was hard not to think we could have done more to protect Beverly. But taking her with us when we fled New Jersey was impossible. There were too many unknowns, and Bev was too young to survive life on the streets. We had to leave my sister, from another mother, behind.

That we were roughing it was an understatement and justified leaving her with the Bryants. But not finding a way to stay in touch with her was a regret I was living with. I hoped getting revenge on our foster father, Bryant, would be a leap in the right direction.

It had to be. What had happened that day haunted me. Mario and I were bouncing a ball off the front steps.

Bev screamed. Mario and I ran into the house and froze.

Terror in her eyes, Bev was hunched down, cowering between the couch and wall. His face red, Bryant towered over her. He took his belt off. "This ain't your house! I pay the goddamn bills around here."

Bev whimpered, "I'm sorry, I'm sorry—"

"You eat when we do!"

Mario said, "She was hungry. Leave her alone."

Bryant held up a fist. "Get the hell out of here!"

I said, "Come on. It was a frigging peanut butter and jelly sandwich!"

Bryant snapped the belt. "Watch your mouth. You're the oldest. You know my rules."

Mario said, "Get away from her!"

"Mind your business, or you're next."

"She didn't do nothing!"

"Shut up before I knock both your heads off."

"Leave Bev alone, you goddamn bully!"

Bryant laughed and struck Bev with the belt. Her screech pierced my ears. I shoved Mario back. "Stay here."

Lowering my head, I charged, ramming into Bryant.

Bryant crashed onto the couch. "You little shit!"

"Run, Bev, run!"

Beverly struggled to her feet.

My head yanked back. Bryant had a handful of my hair. I was heading for the coffee table.

Crack.

A lightning bolt sliced through my head. My hand rocketed to the side of my head.

A growing stream of warm blood flowed over my fingers.

Mario screamed. As my field of vision narrowed, things went black.

Head pounding, I came to. Mrs. Bryant was holding my hand, crying. Her bastard of a husband was talking to the emergency room doctor. "He was running through the house. I told him to stop, and, bingo, he trips, hits his head, and here we are."

"You'd be surprised how many children we treat here. Kids will be kids."

"I know, but this one needs watching; he can be reckless."

"Don't worry, he'll be all right. I'll stitch him up, and he'll be as good as new."

At that moment, I vowed to give him what he deserved. People couldn't get away with being monsters . . .

Mario tapped my arm. "You ready, or what?"

"Yeah. Put your gloves on."

We got out and started walking along Ocean Avenue into Spring Lake, though Bryant usually fished a couple of blocks away. I paused crossing the street. Mario said, "Come on. Let's get this over with."

We kept a steady pace. Mario said, "It's freezing out."

A bead of sweat made its way down my back. I said, "The wind is making it worse."

A sliver of moonlight bounced off the roaring sea. I elbowed Mario. He stopped. I whispered, pointing to a jetty. "Look, it's him."

"Bastard."

Heart pounding, I said, "You think anybody saw us?"

"No." He waved a hand at the darkened homes across the street. "Nobody is around."

We went down the stairs to the beach. In the shadow of the boardwalk, we made our way toward a demon I needed to exorcise.

Steps away from the jetty, Mario motioned to pull down our

ski masks. Doubt crept in as waves battered the rocks. Mario whispered, "You still pushing him in?"

I forced a nod. "You sure he drank enough?"

"It's after twelve; he's got to be bombed."

I stopped. "He don't look it."

"What are you talking about? He's swaying."

"What if somebody sees us?"

"You backing out?"

I climbed on the rocks. "No."

Crouching, we made our way toward Bryant. Our ex-foster father pulled his rod back and cast it.

I slipped on an algae-covered rock and grabbed my ankle. As sea spray washed over us, Mario whispered, "You okay?"

"I twisted it." It was a slight sprain. I got to my feet and applied pressure. I faked a grimace. "I fucked it up bad; we have to go back."

"No, you stay here. I'll handle him."

"No. We can't take a chance."

"Don't worry, I'll push the bastard in. I can't wait to see him drown."

"No! I gotta do it." I pointed behind my ear. "He did this to me!"

Bryant turned around. With the waves crashing on the jetty, there was no way he heard what was said.

I said, "Come on. Let's get out of here."

"No. We came this far. Let me push the fucker in. I don't care if he sees me or not."

"That's talking stupid. I'll come up with a better idea."

I grabbed his arm and pulled him toward the sand.

It was a night I still regretted. Bryant died a year later, taking with him my chance to redeem the lack of courage that has colored my life ever since.

1

THERE'S JUSTICE, AND THEN THERE'S MAKING IT RIGHT—TWO different things. We have a system of justice, but even when it works perfectly, and it rarely does, it's unsatisfying.

Where is the justice in releasing a criminal awaiting trial? Larry Boyd, the man who killed my mother, had been out on bail. Boyd had a rap sheet. A long one. I understand due process, but the scales are out of balance. By a wide margin.

It takes years to put someone on trial. If they're convicted, there are endless appeals, dragging the victim's family through hell. And then there's parole. Everybody deserves a second chance, but the victim doesn't get a do-over; they get shafted. Again.

That's where I come in. I'm what you call a "squarer."

Humans have an insatiable desire for revenge. A visceral need to even the score. It's probably hardwired into our DNA. Even if it's not biological, our emotions demand a response.

People want something done about an injustice, but they rarely take action themselves.

The desire to even the score is understandable, but it's impossible in most cases. If a loved one is murdered, killing the killer may feel good but it doesn't bring your loved one back, and you'll end up in jail. Hence the saying, The best revenge is one that's gone too far.

Is there a better way than an eye for an eye? The people I help know there is.

You're thinking mobster, but it's not about breaking legs or making threats. Many times I work with the police, but there are things they can't or won't do. It's about getting creative with retribution.

We're told the key to happiness is acceptance. Accept life as it is and people as they are, without bitterness, and you'll be free. I don't buy it. Marcus Aurelius lived a long time ago but nailed it, saying, "Justice is the source of all other virtues."

I never admit to anything, but I have to swim in dirty water at times, so the above might be nothing more than justification for what I do. And I'm okay with that; it helps me get through the day.

The burner phone in my pocket was vibrating.

"Where'd you get this number?"

"Mario gave it to me."

"Okay."

"Is this Mr. Beck?"

"Who's asking?"

"Tom, Tom Peterson."

"What do you want?"

"Mario said you could help me. I got screwed."

"Cambier Park. By the sign on Eighth Street. Two o'clock."

"I don't know what you look like."

"I'll find you."

2

A MAN IN CARGO SHORTS AND A GREEN T-SHIRT KEPT SCANNING the street. Five hundred people, in lawn chairs, filled the park. I waited until the music began to emerge from the parking lot.

The Naples Big Band was playing "This Could Be the Start of Something Big." Was it an omen for a big payday?

Peterson jumped when patted on the back. "Mr. . . . Mr. Beck?"

"It's just Beck. Let's take a walk."

"Where are we going?"

I pointed south. "Where it's quieter."

"You live around here?"

"Nice music."

"They're good."

Walking by the tennis courts, I said, "Why'd you reach out?"

He bit his lip. "The bastard killed my wife and didn't spend a day in jail."

I stopped in front of the Norris Center. "Fill me in."

"Marilyn was driving home; she had her hair done downtown, just up the street. She was almost home when this whacko slammed into her. Guy's name is Brett Caden."

"Where did the accident occur?"

"It was no frigging accident; he was drunk. The bastard was high as a kite."

I nodded.

"Marilyn was on Livingston Road, and Caden blew through the light at the Vanderbilt intersection. He hit her broadside." Peterson hung his head. "They say she died instantly, but how do they know?"

"And the other driver?"

"Caden was in one of those frigging Tahoes. They should be against the law, they're so big."

I said nothing.

"He hardly got a scratch."

"Was he arrested?"

He nodded. "But it didn't mean anything. Caden got off."

"The charges were dropped?"

"No, it was a sham trial. Total bullshit. That's why I'm here. Are you going to help me?"

"No promises. I'll look into it."

When people didn't get the results they wanted, many would say the system was rigged. Sometimes it was corruption; other times they were angry and mistaken. My interest was in the ones the system got wrong.

As Peterson got into his car, I crossed the street, stopping in front of city hall. Cigar smoke was in the air as I sent a text to Mario: *Meet me at the country club.*

3

The North Naples Country Club parking lot was nearly full. Happy hour was ninety minutes away, and there was nothing happy about trying to find a spot at that time. Folding the *Florida Weekly* around an envelope, I got out of the car.

The venue's owners had a sense of humor, calling the place a country club. They also displayed funny quips on the sign outside the green building. Today it read, Treat your mother to a Margarita. You're probably the reason she drinks.

The smile it provoked evaporated quickly. It'd been over twenty years, and the memory of Mom's death still stung.

I grabbed a table next to a wall covered with license plates. Cigarette smoke wafted in from the outdoor seating that lined Route 41. The desire for a cigarette was another thing that hadn't faded with time.

Ponytail swinging, a waitress chirped, "What can I get ya?"

"A Tito on the rocks." My brother, from another mother, Mario, was walking through the door. "Make that two."

Mario stuck a fist out for a bump and slid onto a chair. "How's it going, Beck?"

Nodding, I pushed the newspaper to the center of the table.

Mario swept it onto his lap. "That was an easy one."

"Everything is easy until you have to do it yourself."

He smiled.

"This Peterson guy, what's the deal with him?"

"He's got money, owns an Allstate Insurance agency on Bonita Beach Road."

"How'd he find you?"

"Squire's friend told him to call me."

"What friend?"

"Take it easy, Beck."

The waitress set our drinks down and left.

"The deeper the pool, the more drownings."

"Another stoic quote?"

"It's an original."

"How much are you thinking of charging him?"

"Haven't decided." Money was nice, but it wasn't the only motivation.

"It's gotta be a lot. It's a crazy story; the guy who killed his wife walked."

I took a sip of my vodka. "What do you know?"

"You need to talk with Larson, but from what I checked out, the driver got off on technical bullshit. He was drunk; his booze blood levels were over the limit, but—"

A waitress, carrying a tray, passed our table. Mario said, "Man, you see that? Pabst beer. I didn't know they still made it. Remember the time we took some of Bryant's?"

I nodded.

"Man, we were like, what, twelve? As soon as you threw up, he knew. Man, he kicked our asses."

"He never needed a reason to beat us."

"You got that right, brother. If we hadn't stuck together, he would've killed one of us."

I fingered the two-inch scar behind my ear that our foster

father had given me. "Even this wasn't enough for the Jersey Department of Children."

"That's why we had to get the hell out of there."

I shrugged. "I still think of Bev. I hope Bryant left her alone."

"Don't worry. Mrs. Bryant took care of her. She was all right."

"Mrs. B had no balls." As soon as I said it, I knew it was unfair.

"Come on, man. She gave us the money to run away. Old Man Bryant must've given her hell when he found out."

That was true, but not the reason I regretted the unfair comment. "I got to go."

Cabana Dan's hut had been destroyed by Hurricane Ian, but he still rented beach setups from under an umbrella on Vanderbilt Beach. The water had a brownish tinge and was rough, for the Gulf of Mexico.

I threw a chin at the attendant. "Larson here?"

"Yep, got here an hour ago. He's in his usual spot."

Weaving through the throng of beachgoers, I headed to a green sun shelter on the edge of the Ritz Carlton's beach. Tucked in the shade, Larson was asleep on a chaise. I wriggled his big toe.

His eyes sprung open. "Hey, Beck. I guess I dozed off."

Reclining on the chair next to him, I said, "Heard you snoring from my car."

"Another gorgeous day."

"Beginning of February can be dicey. But this one's been unbelievable."

"You're right." He smiled. "I haven't had a chance to use

the fireplace."

"The crazy thing is, more gas fireplaces are sold between here and Sarasota than anywhere else in the country."

"I believe it. There's water in the cooler if you want."

Lifting the lid, I grabbed a San Pellegrino. "Poland Springs beneath you?"

"Sparkling water is refreshing."

"Back in the old days, Ray, you drank tap water." Larson had upgraded after winning a huge personal injury award. A criminal lawyer, he somehow landed a client who'd been injured at a Walmart under renovation. It was a fat payday; the financial security enabled him to do a ten-year stint as an officer with the Collier County Sheriff's Office.

"Old days? You're what, thirty-nine?"

"Close enough."

"Mario is a year younger than you?"

"Yep."

"I was thinking about you the other day. You were the best investigator we ever had."

I shrugged.

"And you didn't have any formal training."

"Living on the streets is underrated."

"Survival is the best teacher."

"Seneca said, 'Anything might happen, so anticipate everything.'"

"You've got to relax. You can't be on guard twenty-four seven."

Easy for him to say. "Mario said you know about Tom Peterson, and his wife's accident."

He wagged his head. "It's a sad case. There's the law, and then there's justice. I'm not surprised Peterson reached out."

A beach ball skittered over. I bounced it back to a kid and said, "Fill me in."

4

Larson swung his legs off the chaise. "His lawyer outsmarted the prosecution. I don't agree with his tactics, but Puzo is a hell of a lawyer."

As a lawyer, he'd know. I dug a rut in the sand with my foot. "Puzo's part of the problem."

"That's up for debate. He's doing what the law allows."

"Mario said something about Puzo using a technicality."

"Caden's blood alcohol level was more than double the legal limit. There was no question he was legally impaired."

"Then why'd he get off?"

"Puzo had the Breathalyzer results thrown out. The county hadn't recalibrated or tested the device in the time frame required."

"How late were they?"

"Just a day or so past the deadline. The county proved it was in working order and gave the testing data to the judge, but it was ruled inadmissible."

"What about the field sobriety tests?"

Larson reached in the cooler. "Puzo attacked them as well.

He argued that Caden failed the field-testing because he had a stress fracture in his left foot."

"He was walking around with a broken foot?"

Larson shrugged. "Puzo is crafty. From what I know, stress fractures don't show up in regular X-rays, and if they do, it's weeks after the fracture. He had medical records from two doctors who were treating Caden. Naturally, Caden came to court wearing a cast."

"You think the fracture was real?"

"Who knows? Puzo works with a bunch of sleazy doctors. Maybe one of them had Caden jumping off a ladder to cause a fracture."

"You think he'd do something like that to generate reasonable doubt?"

Larson shrugged. "That's what he was aiming for, and Caden walked."

"Do you believe Caden was guilty?"

"Yes, but you know that's not what the justice system is about."

"But you said he was over the legal limit and driving drunk."

"That's true, but factual guilt and legal guilt are two separate things. Everyone is presumed innocent until they are proven guilty in a court of law. Someone can be factually guilty but not legally guilty if there is not enough evidence."

"And that's that?"

Larson spread his hands. "Puzo played the system like a virtuoso, and his client walked."

"And the Peterson family got screwed."

Larson stood. "It happens all the time. You want to take a walk?"

"How far you going?"

"Pelican Bay north."

I grabbed another bottle of water. “All right, let’s get moving; I have things that need doing today.”

Larson gave me a look as we walked to the water. “Oh yeah, forgot tomorrow was the sixteenth.”

“It’s okay, man.”

“We should do something tomorrow. You want to go kayaking?”

“No.”

“I’ll come over. We’ll hang out.”

“I have to be by myself.”

“I’ll send someone to check on you.”

I kicked the surf. “I don’t need a babysitter.”

“Promise me you won’t overdo it.”

A wave splashed my ankles. “The water is warm for February.”

I brushed the sand off my feet and jumped in my car.

The Publix parking lot was doing its best impression of a bumper-car ride. I dodged a woman backing out and headed into the store.

The selection of roses was decent. I grabbed two of the best-looking bunches and checked out. I drove down 111th Street, pulled onto an access road, and parked.

A couple sitting on a bench offered nods and tight smiles. A withered birthday balloon was taped to the headstone next to my parents’ grave.

I set the roses on the ledge, lit a cigarette, and closed my eyes. Visualizing Mom was easier, but it wasn’t easy to summon an image of Dad. Dr. Google said it was because of who he’d become after my mother was killed.

Dad always enjoyed tequila, but there was never a fix for

grief at the bottom of a bottle. He drank himself to death, but with a broken heart, he was easy prey.

With nobody to care for me, I was shuffled in and out of foster care. It took me ten years to forgive him.

Anger and the fight to survive had shut down my ability to reason.

But it was clear, the bullet that took my mother's life was also responsible for killing my father and upending my life. The killer, Larry Boyd, had pulled the trigger, but the system was responsible for what happened to my family.

Boyd had been out on bail when he shot Mom. With a prior conviction for deadly assault, why had he been released? There was no way he should have been walking the streets. The clowns running New York City had it backward; they treated criminals like victims, letting them back on the streets within hours of their arrest to terrorize again.

The true culprits were the elites and bleeding hearts who passed laws under the guise of reform, while everyday Joes paid the price in blood.

"Hey, Doc, got a quick question for you."

"Sure, Beck. What's on your mind?"

"I need to understand stress fractures in a foot."

"Well, the second and third metatarsal bones are thin and prone to stress fractures."

"Are they easy to detect?"

"Not particularly. These fractures are often invisible injuries and don't always show signs on the skin's surface. Many times, there is no bruising or swelling."

"Are they painful?"

"They can be. Patients often confuse the pain with other injuries, such as a tendon tear or ligament or muscle sprain."

"Would it affect the way you walk?"

"The pain could cause an alteration of a person's gait."

"Is it possible to give yourself a stress fracture?"

He blinked. "Do you mean purposely?"

"Exactly."

"I don't know why anyone would want to, but sure, you could jump off something, say, six feet high, landing on the part of the foot where you push off to walk. You do that, and you're likely to cause a fracture."

How creative or corrupt was Puzo? Did Caden really have a fracture? Or was it an excuse to cover up his failure on the physical part of the sobriety test? If he had a stress fracture, did Caden give himself one after the accident?

There was no doubt people would do anything to avoid a murder charge, but this situation required imagination and help from professionals. The prosecution, with endless resources, hadn't been able to reveal the truth. Was it a lack of effort or the fact there was nothing to hide?

5

As daylight filtered in through the crack in my eyelids, I clamped them shut and pulled a pillow over my head. The phone continued rattling on the nightstand. It finally stopped and I tried to get back to sleep.

A lawn mower started; the landscapers were here. Rather than fight the Floridian soundtrack, I swung my legs off the bed. Head pounding, I trudged to the bathroom.

Tipping over the Advil bottle, I poured out four and popped them in my mouth. Sucking water from the faucet, I washed them down.

Waiting for relief, I sat on the bed and palmed my phone. Four missed calls from Mario and two from Larson. I scrolled through my text messages. Seeing the second birthday GIF, I swiped it away and went into the kitchen.

Spying the half-empty bottle of Tito's on the coffee table, my stomach somersaulted. I turned the Nespresso machine on. Waiting for it to heat, I emptied an ashtray and swore off alcohol and tobacco.

The dark roast smell lifted my spirits. Sipping it, my phone vibrated. It was Mario. "Hey, are you all right?"

"I'm fine. What's up?"

"You getting a cold?"

"No."

"Your voice sounds like it."

"Just tired, man."

"You want to call me back?"

"Why'd you call?"

"Got a lead on a friend of a friend's mother."

"And?"

"Guy named Bert Hartmann said he'd been screwed out of half his savings by a con man."

"How much he lose?"

"Three hundred K."

"What kinda scam?"

"An investment that went bust."

"How old is this guy?"

"Sixty."

"He wants the money back?"

"I didn't get that far. Figured—"

I checked the microwave clock. It was ten thirty. "Call Yushenko for me. I need an IV to hydrate or I ain't doing anything today."

"Okay. You want to me tell this Hartmann guy it'll be another day?"

"No. Two o'clock. At Bean to Cup."

"Okay. I'll text a picture of him."

Yushenko sauntered into the exam room. He checked the bag hanging from a pole. "Are you feeling any better?"

"Yeah, you can take it out."

"Are you certain?"

I nodded. "Hurry, Doc, I gotta pee like crazy."

Removing the IV from my arm, the doctor said, "Binge drinking is hard on your body. It's highly inflammatory, not to mention the damage you're doing to your liver."

"I don't do it often."

"When the damage is done, no amount of hydration is capable of reversing it."

Digging in my pocket, I peeled off five hundred-dollar bills and pressed them in his hand. "Thanks, Doctor. Have a good one."

I turned off Bayshore Drive into a tiny strip of stores, parked, and got out. I bent down, petting a brown ball of fur whose leash was strapped to a chair. People were careless.

The smell of coffee pulled me in. Bean to Cup had a 1960s' vibe. It just wasn't sure whether it was Greenwich Village or a California beach town. I ordered a cup of java and surveyed the people scattered around the small shop.

Though the scowl on his face didn't match the look on his DMV picture, the monk-like halo of hair did. Hartmann looked in my direction. I nodded and picked up my coffee.

As I slid onto a navy chair, Hartmann said, "Good to meet you."

"Likewise. What's going on?"

"Didn't Mario fill you in? I told him—"

"Nothing beats hearing it firsthand."

He spoke in the hushed tones of an undertaker. "I was scammed out of three hundred thousand by a prick named Dave Engle. He took half of my money. Now I don't have enough to retire on. I'm going to be working my ass off until I'm eighty."

"I need to know what happened."

He hissed, "He bullshitted me. Said it was a good investment, couldn't lose, and I'd double my money in two years."

"What kind of investment?"

"Some kind of metabolism thing. He said their tool would give you information while you were exercising and, you know, optimizing, that's the word he used all the time, optimizing your performance."

"For athletes?"

"No, that was the thing. He said some of the pro teams already use it, and his company was going to bring it to the mass market."

"What's the name of the outfit?"

"Core Analytics."

Fancy name. "So, he told you about this opportunity and you invested?"

"Yeah, he said it was a chance to get in on the ground floor. He said it couldn't miss."

"Did you check the company out?"

"A little bit, but one of my neighbors did some research and said it was legit."

"Did he invest as well?"

"Yeah, but he can afford to lose some money. He made a killing when he sold his company in Michigan."

"How much did he lose?"

"Around the same as me."

"What do you want me to do?"

"I want my money back."

"Give me Engle's details."

"You're going to get my money back?"

I stood. "I'll take a look at the situation."

After taking a gulp, I tossed the rest of my coffee in the trash and stepped outside. A text came in. Larson, my lawyer buddy who had more connections than Con Edison, needed to see me. I hopped in my car and headed to North Naples.

The guard at Pelican Marsh's gate waved me through. Larson lived in the Arbors, one of twenty-odd neighborhoods in the master community. His house was one of the smaller ones on the street but had killer views of a lake and their golf course.

I followed Larson onto the lanai, where a fan spun lazily. We sat at a table anchored by a tray with a sweaty pitcher of iced tea and two glasses.

A pelican skidded onto the lake. I said, "You've got some view."

"It's what attracted me to the property." He smiled. "Last night a family of otters walked right by."

"That must have been cool."

"It was. Pour yourself a cup. I need to get a folder for you."

I filled two glasses and took a sip. It was unsweetened. There was nothing on the tray to make it drinkable.

Larson opened the slider and extended his hand. He was holding two packets of Sweet'N Low. "Almost forgot."

"Thanks." I emptied the fake sugar into my glass.

He sat, laying a folder marked Royal on the table. The dangerous gang leader had proved adept at making money and staying out of prison.

Larson said, "We need to do something about Royal."

"Like what? I heard he's getting off; he didn't do it."

"He's guilty as sin. Rocco leaned on the two men Royal claimed he was with."

"It was a bullshit alibi?"

"Yes. Both were into Royal for over fifty thousand each."

"Royal extends that kind of credit. I've seen it before."

He slid the folder to me. "Royal discharged the debt in exchange for them saying they were watching *Monday Night Football* together at Royal's place."

I skimmed the first page. "He bought himself an alibi. A hundred grand is cheap; Royal is a repeat offender."

"He's a thug. I always knew it, but I didn't think he'd stoop so low and assault Cece."

"Cece is no angel, but the poor woman was in the hospital for weeks. Royal is nothing but a coward."

"We need to let O'Leary know what we discovered."

"This gets out, Royal is going to go nuts. He'll lash out for sure."

"I know. We have to be super careful."

"Who knows about this?"

"As far as I know, just Rocco."

"These my copies?"

"Yes."

I stood. "All right. Leave it with me."

6

LARSON'S FILE WAS VALUABLE, BUT LIKE NUCLEAR MATERIAL, deadly if mishandled. Better to hand it off as quickly as possible.

I made a call but would have to wait; O'Leary was in court prosecuting a drug-trafficking case for Collier County. Flipping open the folder, the edge of a photo peeked out. I pulled three images out, ones I'd taken at the hospital, sending me back to the night of the assault.

Entering Cece's room, I gasped. Cece's swollen face had started to turn purple. One eye was completely closed, and her nose needed a magician, not a plastic surgeon.

She was snoring. I set the flowers on her bed tray. Stomach bubbling, I sat. We weren't close, but I'd had a soft spot for her since Ventura, another lawyer friend, introduced us at one of the only charity events I'd attended.

Ventura was involved with Youth Haven, an organization whose mission was close to my heart. Cece was a model graduate who'd rebuilt her life and exuded confidence. Whether it was contrived or real didn't matter. I wrote a second check to the youth shelter organization after hearing her speak in front of the crowd of donors.

All the progress she had made went to shit when she got mixed up with Royal.

Toby jumped onto the couch. "Hey, boy. Be careful." The file fell to the floor, spilling its contents. A picture of Royal drifted under the cocktail table.

I picked it up and stared at it. Royal had the unblinking eyes of a predator. His penchant for violence made him feared, but it also meant someone would eventually kill him. It was the way the street operated. It would take a couple of years, but the organization he'd assembled would continue. That was also the way crime organizations worked, but his recent collaboration with the Russians meant the fentanyl crisis would explode.

One of the burner cells rang. It was Detective Moreno. "Hey, Mo."

"Yo, Beck. I checked into Engle. He's clean, no record or encounters."

It was unusual for a scamster not to have a brush with the law. "What about any civil suits?"

"I ran both criminal and civil; nothing came up."

"Okay. Thanks. I'm on my way to see Engle, so your timing is perfect."

"Just one of my many strengths."

Chuckling, I said, "Right. Maybe next week, we'll grab a drink."

"Sounds good. See you then."

Water was all you saw from Airport Pulling Road. Lakeside's name fit like Jane Fonda and plastic surgery. Circling the lake, I stopped in front of a building containing four carriage homes.

The decades-old community was in a great location, but if

Engle was a con man, he wasn't very good at it. It took two rings for Engle to answer the door. Dressed on the verge of dishevelment, he said, "What do you want?"

I flipped open an ID wallet. "I'm with the State of Florida's business agency."

"What's this about?"

"You were engaged in selling shares in a, a . . . let me check." I opened my notepad. "Oh, right, a metabolism company. I gotta admit, I don't even know what metabolism is."

"It's all the chemical processes going on in your body."

"Oh, right, yeah. So, what happened?"

"We were too early."

"What do you mean?"

"It's going to be big, I'm telling you."

"But you closed it down. At least, that's what our records show."

He frowned. "I did. We ran out of money. If I'd known it would take more money, I would've waited."

"Help me out here. I'm just a bureaucrat. What was the company supposed to do?"

"It had software that analyzes your blood as you exercise."

"While you're working out? How do you do that?"

"With just a tiny pinprick in your earlobe. It's painless. We take the sample and run it through computers with special software."

"And what does it tell you?"

"What your metabolic levels are, and it generates a report showing how to optimize your workouts. You know, most of the time, we're working too hard for the benefit we get."

"Sounds like a great idea. I mean, people spend so much time at the gym, you might as well do what works."

"Yep, it'll tell you to do more aerobics or more resistance training. It's a game changer. You know, the pros are already using it."

"Wow. How much did you raise?"

"Just over two million, but we needed three times that."

"How many investors did you get?"

"Twenty-plus. I put everything I had in it. I tried to save it but couldn't."

"How much did you lose?"

"Everything I had, almost six hundred thousand."

"Ouch."

"You got that right. And I lost my wife as well."

"She left you because of it?"

He nodded. "Taking the equity out of the house was the last straw."

"Sorry to hear about all this. What are you going to do now?"

He brightened. "AI. I'm working on getting a couple of programmers, you know, for computers, software guys. We got to be able to piggyback on this AI thing. Everything is going that way, and we can ride the wave."

"Artificial Intelligence?"

"Yes. You should get in on this one. It's going to take off."

Con men never speak well. Their skill is listening well, getting enough information to pull someone in. "Really?"

"No doubt. Of all the things I've heard about, my gut is telling me this is going to be a home run, a grand slam."

My cell buzzed. It was prosecutor O'Leary. "Sorry, I got to get this."

I stepped into the sunshine. "Hey, I thought you were in court all day."

"A witness was MIA, and the judge granted the defense a continuance."

"We need to meet."

"What's going on?"

"How about Baker Park in an hour?"

"That works. By the grassy knoll?"

"No. It's too hot. By the picnic tables, they're shaded."

A couple of teens were kicking a soccer ball on the great lawn. Acknowledging how wrong I'd been about soccer becoming a big spectator sport in America, I ducked into the shade.

O'Leary was rolling up his sleeves as he approached. "This has to be the warmest February since I've been here."

"It's eighty-five today."

"Must be global warming."

"Then why was half of January way below normal?"

He smiled. "Global warming."

"Exactly."

"What's going on?"

I slid the file Larson had given me across the table. "Royal bought his alibi."

O'Leary's shoulders sagged. He flopped the file open. "How sure are you?"

"A thousand percent. Rocco got both men to admit they lied. They were up to their eyes in debt to Royal."

"They're willing to recant their sworn statements?"

"Looks that way."

"If they don't, you know, Royal will get off."

"Don't sweat it; this will seal the deal. Royal will finally be off the streets."

"Thanks. I don't know how you do it, Beck."

"It's my calling."

"I'll get on this right away."

"You have to keep me, Larson, and Rocco out of this. Say whatever you have to, but this didn't come from us."

"You have nothing to worry about."

I stood. "I get paid to worry."

7

Pedaling as hard as I could, I hit the halfway mark in just under thirty minutes. I took a pull on my backpack water bottle and turned around.

The heat was tough when I started biking. It was hard to go a couple of miles. Now, twelve miles was a breeze. I thought about Hartmann and the hard-earned money he lost. It was a shame people took risks with their retirement funds. I had one more thing to check out on both Hartman and Engle before determining what I'd do.

The allegation in the Peterson case didn't get more serious. But the key word was allegation. Meeting Caden was going to play a role in assessing the situation. I pedaled away, contemplating a list of the things I needed to do to try to get it right.

I hung up my bike and headed into the house for a shower. Toweling off, my stomach growled. It was time for lunch. I drove to the Riverchase Shopping Center and got out.

Just a few steps away, a boy was perched on his father's shoulders. The dad said, "What do you want to do after we get lunch?"

"Play video games."

"No, let's do something outside. You want to go to the park and play catch?"

"Yeah, okay, or ride bikes. What do you wanna do, Dad?"

"I want to do whatever you want to do."

The blond-haired kid was so cute, I wanted to tag along with them. Time was moving at lightning speed—the window closing on becoming a father.

Thirty-nine wasn't old in today's world, but unless things moved faster than I was comfortable with, I'd be in my mid-forties if I'd ever become a father.

The latest age I promised myself to stretch it to was fifty. The self-absorbed Hollywood clowns fathering children in their seventies disgusted me.

On our second date, Laura said Al Pacino was going to be a father at the age of eighty-three. We had a good laugh about it. But it wouldn't be funny to his six-year-old. Pulling the door open to a sandwich shop, I remembered Laura was thirty-one and put my order in.

She had a great laugh and seemed easygoing. While waiting for lunch, I pulled my phone out to call her for another date. This time, no double-dating with Mario. It was important to see what she was like without distractions.

As I was handed my sandwich, my phone pinged with a text: *Problem just cropped up. Need to see you ASAP.*

I typed back: *OK. Walmart parking lot off Immokalee.*

C U in fifteen.

The timing worked. I took my Firehouse sub to a table, ate half, and headed across the street.

I got into O'Leary's car. "What's going on?"

"The Royal case."

"Don't tell me they backed out."

"No, we brought Carlton and Brown in this morning, and

they recanted. They were scared Royal was going to get revenge, so we brought them into protective custody."

"And?"

"We were reviewing everything before turning over the recant statements to the defense, and Bilcher tells us he had made Carlton and Brown an offer to turn state's evidence in exchange for dropping the charges pending against them."

"He did what?"

"It was just bait to see if they were telling the truth or not when we heard they were Royal's alibi."

"Is it going to be a problem?"

"I'm afraid it is. The defense will argue they recanted in exchange for a deal to drop the charges."

I shook my head. "Royal can't get off again. He beat the hell out of Cece."

"I know it, and you know it, but I'm afraid these witnesses recanting isn't going to do it. Royal's lawyers will take the Bilcher offer and use it to create reasonable doubt in the jury's mind."

"Damn it! I was sure this was good enough."

"And it would be, if Bilcher hadn't gone and baited them."

"You know how rare it is to get someone to admit their testimony was bullshit?"

"I know. I'm sorry. I had no idea. What you gave us was gold, but it's not going to cut it this time."

"You're sure Royal's lawyers will trash the recants?"

"No doubt. The judge may not even allow it to be entered as evidence."

"Geez. I can't believe it."

"I know it's crazy to ask, but is there anything else you can do to help us?"

"I don't know right now. I got to think this over. Maybe there's something I can dig up."

"The trial is next week."

"Nothing like a little pressure."

"I'm sorry, but it is what it is."

"We have to be careful here. Royal gets wind of my involvement, he'll come after me with everything he has."

"Don't worry, I didn't say anything about where I got the info from."

I stood. "I'll be in touch."

8

THE PAINTER WAS COMING OUT OF MY HOUSE. I PULLED alongside his truck and slid the window down. “Hey, there. You almost finished?”

“We’re done, Mr. Beck. We did the rest of the trim today.”

“Nothing else needs to be painted?”

“Nope. The job is done.”

Opening the car door, I said, “Great.”

“Be careful, the baseboard in the master is still wet. Give it a couple of hours.”

“Sure.” I held out a pair of hundred-dollar bills. “Here, this is for you.”

“That’s not necessary, sir.”

“I know. Just wanted to say thanks for being there when I needed you.”

The cash disappeared into his pocket. “Thanks.”

It’d taken four months to get my place back in order after Hurricane Ian. That was better than most; many homes in Park Shore were still in various stages of renovation. I’d gotten the contractor from my lawyer pal, Larson, and you had to protect your contacts.

A rubbery smell hit me when I walked inside. I opened a slider and humidity rushed in. Surveying the shiny lake, the doorbell rang. Mario was here.

"Painters wrapped up?"

"Yep, all that's left is the smell."

"That's turpentine. It'll be gone in an hour."

"Look, I just went to see O'Leary. There's a problem."

"With Royal?"

I updated Mario and said we needed to dig up something.

"Damn. I didn't expect that."

"Seneca said, 'The person who has anticipated the coming of troubles takes away their power when they arrive.'"

"I guess so."

"You guess so? Think about it. If you're prepared and have considered all the alternatives, when something happens, you've eliminated the surprise factor and can deal rationally with it."

"You're really into those old philosophers."

"They knew what they were talking about." But one piece of their advice, "You can choose courage or comfort, but you can't have both," trailed me closer than my shadow.

"It's different times now."

"The principles are timeless."

"They didn't even have electricity back then. What did they know about living in a modern society?"

"How about the importance of justice? They said it's the most important virtue. What we do to obtain it for others is important."

He shrugged. "I'm not like you. It feels good to do this stuff, but at the end of the day, I'm in it for the money."

"Money, money, money—"

"What? Money isn't important?"

"I consider seeking justice my duty to others and society in general."

"Yeah, yeah, whatever. What needs to be done with Royal?"

"Something to prove his alibi is bullshit."

"Maybe I can dig up where Royal was."

"No. He's too slick. Focus on Carlton and Brown. If we can prove they weren't with Royal when the assault occurred, a jury will buy their recants."

"I'll look into them."

"You have to be extra careful."

"I'm always careful."

"This is different. If Royal gets a whiff of this, he'll come after us."

"Don't worry. Besides, he'll go after the guys who turned on him."

"I'm hearing they're in protective custody."

"Royal's got a long reach."

"I know. Look, we don't have much time; the trial is next week."

"All right, I'll see what I can do."

"I'm counting on you."

He stood. "We'll see. I'll call if I get something."

"Not *if*, you *have* to get something."

Mario tilted his head. "Have I ever let you down?"

He had. "This one is a biggie."

"So was getting us ID."

He always brought up what he did, to sneak us out of foster care. "I know, but that was different."

Mario tapped a cigarette out of a pack. "I deliver when it counts."

I stopped myself from asking for a smoke. "Okay. And don't forget, this has got to be kept quiet. No one can know we're behind this."

"I got that. Hey, where are you at with Peterson? He called me twice."

"Guys like Peterson crack me up. They don't have the balls to do anything, but as soon as they talk to me, they expect a miracle."

"Take it easy. You know how it goes."

"Do I ever."

"Peterson's got money, and what happened to his wife is a frigging nightmare."

"It seems that way."

"What do you want me to tell him?"

"That I'm looking into it, seeing what I can get on this guy Caden, but don't make him any promises."

Mercato was busy, forcing me to park in the last row of the parking lot. Crossing the main drag, opposite Bravo, my gaze settled on a guy in dirty jeans and a baseball cap. He was watching kids play on the artificial grass.

I paused at the corner before discounting the possibility he was going to snatch a child. There were too many people around.

Hartmann was sitting in the shade of the Narrative Coffee Roasters, shoveling something into his mouth. He dug his spoon into a mound of ice cream as I sat across from him.

He said, "You should grab one of these; they make the best here."

"I don't eat sweets."

His eyebrows arched. "What? How can you not?"

No sense in responding.

Hartmann set his spoon down. "You checked out that scam artist?"

"I looked into Engle."

"Good. When am I going to get my money back?"

"The company you invested in went belly-up. You're not going to get anything back."

Hartmann stiffened. "He stole my life savings."

"You didn't do your homework."

"What are you talking about? Engle tricked me."

"And how did he do that?"

"I told you, he said this metabolism thing was a sure thing. Said I was going to triple my money in a year. Bastard was lying the whole time."

He'd previously said the hope was to double his money. "Did you do any due diligence?"

"What do you mean?"

"Did you verify the company's situation, the market, its potential, and the risks associated with the investment?"

"A lot of people invested—"

"Did you vet anything Engle said?"

His shoulders sank. "I trusted him."

"Why?"

He silently shrugged.

"You were greedy."

"No, no, that's not true. He scammed me."

"Engle is a dreamer, not a con artist."

"He's a fraudster. I want my money back."

"There's nothing I can do."

"But I need the money. It's all I got."

I stood. "You should've thought about that before putting it on a roulette wheel."

"Where are you going? I paid that guy Mario; you got to help me."

"You made a mistake—a big one. You should've done your homework." I took a step away.

He said, “Hold on. I’ll give you half of what you get back from Engle.”

I turned around. “Look, you screwed up. Make sure you learn from it.”

9

Another neighborhood slammed by Ian's storm surge was Conners at Vanderbilt Beach. Most of the homes in the bayfront community off Vanderbilt Drive had been flooded. Unscathed was the elevated, impressive house Brett Caden called home.

Brett was childless and had divorced his second wife two years ago. I rolled by his coastal contemporary place. It was huge for one man. I drove to the end of the short street, reaching the bay, and turned around.

Creeping back up the block, Caden's door opened. He stepped out and headed down the stairs. I pulled over a house away.

Holding what looked like a bottle of Heineken, Caden went to his mailbox. It was empty. He took a swig and looked in my direction.

Sticking my hand out, I rolled forward, stopping at his home. "Nice house you got there."

The only thing marring Caden's college-quarterback build was a small paunch. "Yeah, designed it myself."

"You're an architect?"

He took a sip of beer. "No. I mean, I had to use one, technically, but the floor plan and elevations were all my ideas."

"You must be creative."

"It's not that hard."

"You didn't get any damage from Ian?"

Running a hand through his crow-black hair, he said, "Zippo."

"Wow. You had good timing, raising the house and all."

"I saw it coming a mile away. They told me I didn't have to build it up so high, but I knew we'd get hit sooner or later."

Zoning and building rules dictated heights, not anyone's clairvoyance. "Well, you did a great job. It looks like your garage is even raised. You get any water in there?"

He scoffed. "They said I was throwing money away by raising the garage, but I'm a car guy and wanted my babies out of harm's way."

"Smart move. What kind of cars do you like?"

"If they don't speak Italian, I don't drive them."

I laughed. "A buddy of mine loves them too. What do you have?"

"A couple of Lamborghinis, the Countach and the Aventador; three Ferraris, an Aperta, a 788 GTS, and a F8 Spider; and to run around town I've got a Maserati, the Quattroporte model."

He was speaking another language, but it meant they were premium models. My contacts said Caden liked expensive cars, but this was over the top. "Nice. My friend has a Lambo, a Ferrari, and a bunch of others. He's trying to convince me to buy one."

"Why not? You can't take your money with you."

"I know."

"They're fun to drive, but I enjoy just looking at them in my garage. They're not garage queens; I drive them. Bottom line is, they're works of art."

"They certainly are."

His manicured hands were good at pointing out how amazing he was. "And I never lose money on them. In fact, I've sold every one for more than I paid for it."

"My buddy said the same thing. You know, talking to you may have pushed me over the edge." It'd be a conspicuous upgrade from my Audi A5.

"Go for it. You won't regret it. Trust me, you'll be hooked for life."

"You're probably right. Sometimes I go with my friend to rallies, and everybody has more than one. There's all kinds of cars at these things. Some, I never saw before. You ever go to them?"

"I used to, but the last year or so I was pretty tied up. I have to get back into things." The accident and trial had sucked his time dry. "Who knows? Maybe I'll see you at the next one in my new ride."

"That's a deal." I stuck my hand out. "My name's Beck."

"Brett Caden, good to meet you."

"Same here. I'll see you around."

I stopped at Vanderbilt Drive, opened the glove box, took a burner phone out, and called Mario.

"Hey, I just ran into Caden."

"What's he like?"

"If you looked up the word smug, there'd be a picture of him."

Mario snickered. "That bad, huh?"

"I'm going to need a copy of the transcript from Caden's trial."

"No problem. I'm on it."

"Thanks."

"You going to be around in the morning?"

"You got something on Royal?"

"Not yet, but I got something working."

"Time is running out."

"You around?"

"I have to go."

I'd never forget my de facto brother, Mario; he got us out of foster-family hell before we aged out, but he asked too many questions.

I punched in another number. Legal-eagle Larson answered before the second ring. "What's going on?"

"I'm going to be sending you a trial transcript."

"Concerning who?"

"The guy we talked about at the beach."

"Okay."

"Can you look it over as soon as you get it?"

"Will do."

"Good. It'll be in your box within an hour."

"I'll look out for it."

"If I stop by around six, does that work?"

"Sure. I can grill a couple of steaks."

"That's all right. I can't stay."

"Come on. All the years we've worked together, you never stayed for a barbecue."

"I'll see you later."

10

MELISSA LARK LIVED IN BEAR'S PAW COUNTRY CLUB. Driving through the old neighborhood, I pulled in front of a brown building.

Lark was thin and pale. Was she sick or in desperate need of a dose of the vitamin D the sun dispensed for free?

"Come in. Would you like coffee? I just made a pot."

I figured her to be about sixty. "No, thanks."

New granite countertops couldn't disguise the need to update the unit. We sat at a glass table with a dolphin base.

"Mario told me about your dog, but I'd like you to tell me everything that went on."

She frowned. "I really miss Frannie. The place feels empty without her."

"What happened to her?"

Her eyes narrowed. "Tommy, my ex, he killed her."

"Are you sure?"

"No doubt in my mind. Frannie got real sick right after he came over to get his stupid baseball cards. What grown man collects baseball cards?"

"Tell me about your dog."

"Frannie was throwing up, so I took her to Gulf Shore Animal Hospital. The vet said she was poisoned and there was nothing they could do. I had to put her . . . down." Her eyes teared up, and she dabbed them with a napkin. "I'm sorry."

"That's okay. I know it's hard."

"You have a dog?"

I nodded. "Toby, he's a poodle-and-terrier mix."

"Aw. He sounds cute. How long you have him?"

"Why do you think it was your ex who poisoned her?"

"Frannie never went outside alone. She was always on a leash. I mean, she couldn't have eaten something. I would've seen it."

"What about drinking some standing water? Sometimes it contains bacteria that's deadly to dogs."

"That's what I thought at first, but when I got home, I went to take the garbage out, and my friend Lisa, she called as I was walking to the garage where the trash can is. As I took the cover off, I swung the bag in and dropped my phone right in with the garbage. It slid along the side to the bottom. So, I had to reach in. I moved two bags, and then I saw it."

"The phone?"

"No, a box of rat poison. Tommy tried to hide it, and he almost got away with it."

"Did the vet say what he thought killed her?"

"When I found the box, I called them right away and asked if it was rat poison. The vet said it was more than likely, if not definite, that that was what killed her."

"And the trash can with the poison, it was in your garage?"

"Yes."

"Who else has access to it?"

"The garage? No one, just me. Who else would be in my garage?"

"Did you have any other visitors?"

"No, just Tommy came over. It had to be him. He never liked Frannie."

"Your ex is a weak man."

"What?"

"Give me his address and where he works."

She got a pad, jotted down the information, and passed the note to me.

"What is Ray's on the Bay?"

"A restaurant."

"What's your ex do there?"

"He owns it."

"Hmm."

"What?"

"Does he have any partners?"

"Not anymore. He bought them out with the money I had to pay him for my half of this place."

I stood. "Okay."

"How much is your, uh, fee for this?"

"It's on me."

"Really? Why?"

"What your ex did was sickening."

She grimaced. "What are you going to do to him?"

"Can't say."

"I, I, uh, don't want him hurt, you know."

"Let me handle it."

"How will I know you did something?"

"You'll know."

11

Slowing, I hit the garage door opener. Laura said, "This is a nice house. I'm impressed. How long have you been living here?"

"A couple of years."

"You know, we've been dating for, like, two months, and this is the first time you invited me over."

"It's easier to go out."

"But you said you enjoy cooking."

I reached in the back, grabbing a Whole Foods bag. "Can you grab the last one?"

"No problem."

I set the groceries on the counter. "I'm going to put the grill on; I'm starving."

"You want me to put a pot of water on for the lobster?"

"No. I'm going to grill them. Put away whatever needs to be in the fridge."

The ignition clicked a dozen times before the grill fired up. I lowered the top, watched a golfer tee off, and went back into the house.

"You okay with eating outside? It's so nice out."

"Sure. Whatever you want."

Laura was easygoing and low-maintenance. "Whatever I want?" I smiled.

She jutted out her hip. "Don't be a bad boy."

I leaned into her. "Is there any other kind?"

"I thought you were starving."

My cell buzzed as I said, "In more ways than one."

She slipped away as I answered it. It was Mario. "Hey, just wanted to let you know I sent over what you wanted."

"Okay, thanks."

"You want to grab a drink later?"

"Can't, Laura is over."

"Wow. Moving right along, are we?"

"Bye, Mario."

I pocketed the phone and Laura said, "How long have you been friends with Mario?"

"A long time."

"You grew up together?"

"Kind of."

"What do you mean? Either you did or you didn't."

"Where'd you put the lobster-tails?"

"In the fridge."

Opening the refrigerator, I said, "Grab the olive oil. It's in the pantry. And paprika and garlic salt. They're in the spice drawer, by the dishwasher."

"A man never made me dinner before."

She set the bottles down as I cut the shell. "You'd make a good sous-chef. Get a little bowl from under the stove and pour some olive oil in it. There should be a brush there too."

"Where'd you live before here?"

"A couple of places."

"Where?"

"Shake some paprika and garlic salt in the oil."

I basted the lobster-tails with the oil and headed out to the lanai. After placing them on the grill, I came back inside. Laura was in the family room holding a framed picture.

I said, "Be careful with that."

"Is this your mother?"

I took the image out of her hand. "Yes."

"She was beautiful. She died?"

No, Mom didn't die—she was killed. I nodded.

"I'm sorry. When?"

"A long time ago."

"When you were a baby?"

"I don't want to talk about it."

"It must have been tough. Were you very close?"

"Did you hear me or what?"

"Why are you so sensitive about it? It's good to talk about things like this."

Picture in hand, I stormed outside. "Get me a plate for the tails."

Clearing the table was easier than clearing the air. Loading the dishwasher, Laura said, "I heard about this new series on Netflix. It's supposed to be really twisty. You want to watch it?"

"I have a couple of documents I have to read for work."

"Why can't you do it tomorrow?"

"It's important. We have a deadline."

"You never talk about your job. What do you do?"

"Security."

"For who?"

"I can't talk about it."

"You won't talk about your family, your job—"

"I've got work to do. I can't do this now."

"Now? You never want to—"

"Come on, Laura. I got business to attend to."

"Fine. If that's the way you want to handle things, I'm leaving."

"How you going to get home?"

"I'll Uber it."

"Here's my keys, take my car. I'll catch up with you later."

"No. I'm Ubering it."

As she grabbed her pocketbook, I said, "Fine, take an Uber. Do what you want."

After putting a password in, I took a fob out and generated an authentication code. I signed on to my VPN, navigating to ProtonMail. Mario's email was the only one in the inbox of the anonymous email service. Attached to it was the Caden trial transcript.

The prosecution presented three witnesses, proving it was Mr. Caden's vehicle that crashed into Mrs. Peterson's auto. Then they went on to building the case that Caden had been drunk when the accident occurred.

Prosecutor Klein questioned the arresting officer, Tom Haber, for a good fifty pages, methodically closing the noose around Caden's neck.

He finally said he had no further questions, and William Puzo, Brett Caden's lawyer, took over:

CROSS EXAMINATION

BY WILLIAM PUZO

"Officer Haber, you were the first to respond to the unfortunate accident involving my client and Mrs. Peterson?"

"Yes, sir."

"In your testimony, as soon as the emergency medical personnel arrived to care for Mrs. Peterson, you stated that you approached Mr. Caden."

"I did."

"You testified that he was standing by his car."

"Yes."

"Was that because he didn't try to help Mrs. Peterson?"

"No, I told him to stay there."

"So, Mr. Caden was following your orders, waiting patiently as the first responders tended to Mrs. Peterson? Not because he was callous or 'out of it,' as the prosecutor, Klein, insinuated."

"Yes."

"When you approached Mr. Caden, minutes later, as you previously stated, what did you do?"

"I questioned him and closely observed him as he performed sobriety tests."

"Was he cooperative?"

"Yes."

"And how did Mr. Caden do on these tests?"

"He failed both walking in a straight line and standing on one leg."

"What about reciting the alphabet?"

"I didn't administer that one."

"Why?"

"Once he failed the physical test, it was time to administer a Breathalyzer."

"And did Mr. Caden resist taking one?"

"No."

"Thank you, Officer Haber. No further questions. Your witness."

REDIRECT EXAMINATION

ASSISTANT DISTRICT ATTORNEY ANDREW KLEIN

"Thank you, Officer Haber. The Breathalyzer test you administered to Mr. Caden on the night of the accident, what was the reading?"

"0.27."

"And the legal limit is?"

"0.10."

"Would you say that Mr. Caden was severely impaired?"

OBJECTION

WILLIAM PUZO

"Objection. Calls for speculation."

COURT

"Sustained."

ASSISTANT DISTRICT ATTORNEY ANDREW KLEIN

"Officer Haber, an alcohol blood level of 0.27, is that considered driving under the influence?"

"Yes."

"Thank you, that's all I have. If the defense has no objection, we'd like to ask the court for a brief recess."

"We have no objections."

Nothing interesting developed after they reconvened, and the prosecution rested its case. And it sure looked solid.

I knew Puzo had saved the day, but regardless of the legal outcome, I was interested in whether Caden was guilty.

I kept reading.

12

DEFENDANT MOUNTS DEFENSE

WILLIAM PUZO: "The defense would like to call Lieutenant Robert Baxter to the stand."

THE CLERK: "Raise your right hand."

Baxter was sworn in, and I visualized Puzo, in his sharkskin suit, sauntering up to the witness.

LIEUTENANT ROBERT BAXTER

Called as witness on behalf of the defense for Brett Caden, having been first duly sworn in, was examined and testified as follows:

DIRECT EXAMINATION

BY WILLIAM PUZO

"Lieutenant Baxter, what are your responsibilities with the Collier County Sheriff's Office?"

"Well, I have several; everybody wears a couple of hats these days."

"Specifically, as it pertains to your duties managing the equipment used in the field by the men and women of the Collier County Sheriff's Office."

"Well, I'm in charge of some of the gear the department uses."

"And would that include Breathalyzers?"

"Yes."

"Does that include the specific unit used by Officer Haber to test Mr. Caden?"

"It does."

"These machines are sensitive, are they not?"

"Yes, they are."

"And Breathalyzers must be regularly maintained."

"Yes. They need to be recalibrated on a regular basis."

"And how regular is that?"

"Once a month."

"Lieutenant Baxter, would you look at this document, marked A 17? Do you recognize it?"

"Yes."

"Please explain the document to the jury."

"Well, it's a recalibration and inspection certification for a Breathalyzer."

"And what does the certificate attest to?"

"That the unit had been recalibrated and is in good working order."

"And what is the date of the certification?"

"August 28."

"Here is another recalibration and inspection certificate, marked A 18. Please compare the serial numbers on both."

"They're the same number."

"So, this is another certification for the same Breathalyzer unit?"

"Yes."

"And what is the date of that certification?"

"October 4."

"Here is state's evidence document P 14. It's Officer

Haber's report. Please tell the court if the serial number on the Breathalyzer he administered matches those on the two certifications."

"They match."

"So, is it the same unit on all three documents?"

"Yes."

"What was the date of the accident these proceedings are covering?"

"September 30."

"Moments ago, you testified that these units are tested once per month. Was the unit in question tested in September?"

"No."

"Florida Administrative Code 11 D-8.006(1) requires that a police agency's inspector must perform specific regulatory inspections on all evidential breath-testing machines at least once every calendar month. Are you aware of the regulation?"

"Yes."

"The fact the unit used to determine if Mr. Caden was driving under the influence was not regularly maintained renders it completely unreliable. Doesn't it?"

"No. We were just a couple of days past due. There was nothing wrong with that unit."

"Objection, Your Honor. I'd like to ask the court to strike that from the record."

JUDGE WILKINS: "Sustained. Members of the jury, you are to disregard the last statement made by Lieutenant Baxter."

PUZO: "Thank you, Your Honor. Now, Lieutenant Baxter, using a simple yes or no, was the Breathalyzer used on Mr. Caden maintained as required by law?"

"No."

"Thank you. The defense makes a motion to suppress the Breathalyzer results from evidence."

JUDGE WILKINS. "So moved. Members of the jury, you

must ignore the Breathalyzer report introduced by the State of Florida."

"Thank you, Your Honor. The defense makes a motion to dismiss the charges on the basis of a lack of evidence."

JUDGE WILKINS. "I want to see both counsels in my chambers. This court is in recess."

I stood, stretching my back. It wasn't definitive, but the chances the device malfunctioned because it was a couple of days past the mandated recalibration were slim. It may have been a bit inaccurate, but Caden's reading was high. Even if was cut in half, he was still impaired.

I read the rest of the transcript, jotting down a name for follow-up. It would be the deciding factor in whether I'd advocate for Tom Peterson.

13

I SWUNG ONTO GOLDEN GATE PARKWAY. A MILE LATER, I turned right into the parking lot for Center Point Community Church. Mario was standing outside his car.

He hopped in, and we got back on the road. I asked, "The Royal trial starts in two days. You going to have something?"

"Stop worrying, I got it covered."

"Is it going to be enough?"

"You're going to love it."

"Did you make sure it can't be traced to us?"

"Everything is handled."

"How much is it going to cost me?"

He scoffed. "Now who's asking too many questions?"

The smirk on his face evaporated from the glare I sent his way. "Get ahold of Peterson and tell him my fee is going to be three hundred thousand. Cash."

"Whoa, three hundred?"

"That's right. I'm cooking up an elaborate plan, and it's going to cost a lot more than usual."

"More than what Wilson cost?"

"Almost double that one."

"Wow."

"We're almost there."

Santa Barbara Boulevard was deserted.

Mario said, "When did they build those apartment buildings?"

"Multifamily places are popping up like overnight pimples."

I turned onto a gravel road and Mario said, "You going to tell me what this guy did already?"

"He killed his ex-wife's dog."

"What?"

"He poisoned it with rat poison."

"That's one sick bastard."

"Sure is."

"What are you planning to do?"

"You'll find out soon enough."

The trailer bounced as we winded our way through a wooded area. Our headlights lit up a mobile home. As we rolled to a stop in front of the weathered shelter, Mario asked, "Who lives here?"

I got out and grabbed a handful of gravel. "Come on."

A dog barked as we approached the light-blue motor home. Its door swung open. Flashlight in hand, a man in a Grateful Dead T-shirt and cutoffs said, "How you doing, my man?"

All of us fist-bumped. "Good, Billy. You got it ready?"

"Follow me. It's out back."

A pen full of chickens stirred. He shined the light ahead. A large box, covered with a blanket, sat on a picnic table.

I sniffed the air. Billy scoffed. "You won't get nothing."

"I hope you're right."

"Keep it as steady as you can and leave it covered until you're ready."

"Okay. Is it all right if we drive up here to load it?"

"Sure thing."

Mario said, "What's in there?"

"Back up the trailer."

Mario left and Billy said, "Whatcha gonna do with it?"

"How much I owe you?"

"Four hundred, if you bring it back. If not, two grand."

"Why so much?"

"Most probably it'll die if it don't get back to where it came from."

I peeled off a bunch of hundred-dollar bills. "We'll bring it back, but here's a thousand. Make sure you keep this quiet."

"Always, my man."

We loaded the crate on the trailer and got in the car. I gently pulled forward. "It's two o'clock. We should be there in twenty minutes."

"Where? Where the hell are we going, and what are we hauling?"

"Ray's on the Bay."

"The place on the Isles of Capri?"

I nodded and pulled onto Collier Boulevard.

"Tony works there, right?"

"Uh-huh."

"What—"

"Enough with the questions."

I shut the headlights off and drove down a street with water on both sides of the road. Ray's on the Bay sat on a semicircle of land at the end. Parking by a stand of mangroves, I grabbed a duffel bag from the rear seat and got out.

Mario said, "This place have an alarm or cameras?"

"No alarm. Tony knocked out the cameras and left a door open."

I tugged on the first slider, and it slid open. Tossing Mario a bag of plastic clothing, I said, "Put this on." We pulled on the rubbery apparel and donned face masks. "Be careful with the case."

"But—"

"Just do what I say."

As we carried the crate, the weight inside it kept shifting. We set it down inside the restaurant. I said, "Stand outside and be ready to shut the slider once I'm outside. You gotta be quick."

I looked over my shoulder. Mario was in position. I grabbed the handle to the crate's door, and in a sweeping motion, pulled it and the blanket off. I ran outside and Mario slammed the door shut.

"Holy shit! A freaking skunk?"

The mammal was sniffing between the stools lining the bar.

Reaching into my pocket, I took out the gravel. "Slide it open and shut it as soon as I toss it."

I threw a handful near the skunk, and it skittered toward a serving station, emitting a spray of rotten eggs. I tossed the remaining stones. "That should do it."

Mario chuckled, "This is one of the best ones we ever did."

"You can't mess with Mother Nature."

"They won't be able to get the smell out of there for months."

"Four to six months, if they're lucky. Get the bag on the trailer."

Mario looked in the bag. "What the hell is this?"

"Honey, peanut butter, bread, stuff skunks like to eat."

"We going to leave it outside to draw him out?"

"No, put it in the crate and wait for him to get trapped again."

"No way. Just leave the door open, and let's get the hell out of here."

I said, "We can't. The skunk will die if it's out of his element."

"What are you, a ranger now?"

"Put the food in the crate."

He drew a big breath and stepped inside. I did the same, taking a piece of paper out of my pocket. Mario tossed the contents of the bag into the crate, and I laid the note on the bar. We hustled outside, sliding the door behind us.

Gasping for air, Mario said, "What'd you put on the bar?"

"A message for the owner."

"What'd it say?"

"A quote from Seneca, 'All Cruelty Springs from Weakness.'"

He shook his head. "Look, the skunk is going back in."

Shutting down my desire to celebrate, I said, "Let's lock him up and get the little guy back to Billy."

14

It was after 2:00 p.m., time for my afternoon java jolt. I filled a glass with ice and popped a pod in the Nespresso machine. As it started dripping, Mario called on a burner.

"Hey, hurry. Turn on the news."

"The news?"

"Yeah, *WINK*. Quick, before you miss it. It's about to come on. Call me back."

I clicked the remote and put on the local station. They were coming back from a commercial break.

The newscaster smiled. "Here's the unusual story we promised you." A picture of Ray's on the Bay filled the screen. It was my time to smile.

"When the owner of a popular restaurant on the Isles of Capri came to work this morning, he was greeted by an overpowering smell. Ray's on the Bay had a visitor during the night, and it wasn't a paying customer. It was a skunk.

"At this time, it's unknown how the little critter gained entry, but while he was there, he sprayed the eatery with his trademark, unpleasant smell.

"Our Melissa Carthage spoke to the owner a few moments ago."

A young lady in a white top smiled for the camera. "I'm here with Tom Lark, the proprietor of Ray's on the Bay. Mr. Lark, you had quite a surprise this morning."

As the owner spoke, I ran a forefinger over the scar behind my ear.

"We sure did. I knew something was wrong as soon as I got out of the car."

"From the smell?"

"Yeah, you can't miss that stench."

"Do you have any idea how the skunk was able to get inside your restaurant?"

"We don't know how he sneaked in, but we've got a pest control company coming to plug any holes he might have squeezed through."

"As skunks do, he left behind a strong smell. How long will it be before diners are willing to chance coming back?"

He didn't mention the note or gravel we threw to scare the critter. Would he piece it together and change his behavior?

Lark said, "We've been told it can take three to six months, but I've contracted with a remediation company who is going to do their best to shorten that timeline."

"That's a long time to be closed."

"It is. We were only shut after Hurricane Ian for about ten days. If it goes on for more than two months, we may have to permanently close."

"Did you ever expect something like this to happen?"

"No way. We've never even had an alligator on the property. It's hard to believe the damage a skunk can cause. I'll tell you, running a restaurant is tough enough without having to worry about wildlife. I mean, how do you prepare for something like this?"

As the news went back to the studio newscaster, I burst out laughing. Did they have skunks in ancient Rome? Either way, even Seneca couldn't have predicted what we orchestrated.

I called Mario back. "Hey."

"Did you see it?"

"Yeah. Man, that was sweet. You think the bastard made the connection?"

"I think he did, but either way, this one is up there in the top ten."

"It felt really good. I just hope he isn't forced to close for good."

"Why? He deserves it."

"Yeah, but the people who work there had nothing to do with what that jerk did."

"You're right. Hey, me and Susan are going to see Tower of Power tonight. She's got two extra tickets. You and Laura want to come?"

"Uh, I don't think so."

"Why not? You love Tower of Power."

"We had a bit of a fight."

"So? Call her up and patch things up."

"I don't know. She's getting too clingy."

"Oh. I thought you said she was cool."

"She is, but we need a break or something. What about that friend of Susan's, the one with the long blonde hair?"

"Which one?"

"The girl who works at the dermatology place."

"How did you know Karen works there? You getting Botox?"

"Yeah, right. See if she wants to go. I don't want to be a tagalong."

"It's going to be a great show."

"Let me know."

"Will do."

I got my regular cell and checked my messages. Nothing from Laura. I typed one to her: *Hey, how are you doing?*

I stared at the screen, hoping for a quick reply. Nothing came in. I tried to hold on to the emotional high from the skunk episode, but it was like trying to hold water in my hand.

Finishing my iced coffee, the phone rang. I scooped it up. "Hey, there."

A baritone voice bellowed, "If you know what's good for you, you'll mind your own fucking business."

"What?"

"You heard me."

"Who is this?"

Click.

I hit redial; it was a private number with a message that the mailbox hadn't been set up.

Was there a way to trace this? I'd ask my law enforcement contacts for help, but before I made that call, I rifled through my mental Rolodex. Of all the jobs I'd worked in the last couple of months, no one involved would have lashed out.

I stiffened. Except one.

Was this related to our search for something to put Royal away for a long time? Intimidation was his style, and if that didn't work, he followed with violence.

But we'd been careful, we always were. Our network never sprang leaks. Larson had a Teflon quality to him, and I'd learned from him, forcing Mario to adopt the same layered approach.

My shoulders relaxed. We'd already dumped on Royal. The information had been turned over. The caller said to keep out of their business. Maybe Royal didn't know we'd gotten something. He had long tentacles, but my system had proved to be waterproof.

I felt myself smiling. Last week I was shopping in Trader Joe's. Reaching for a box of cereal, I heard my name.

"Is that you, Beck?"

It was my old next-door neighbor when I lived in Kensington. "Hey, how are you, Marilyn?"

She frowned. "I'm hanging in there."

"Is everything all right?"

"My sister, Genna, you remember her?"

"Of course. We met a bunch of times."

"She loved your Toby. How is he?"

She'd watched my dog when I traveled overnight. "He's doing great. What about your sister?"

"She passed away about two months ago."

"I'm so sorry. Was she sick?"

"Stomach cancer. It got ugly, but she's out of pain now."

"It's never easy. Dealing with loss." And I knew.

"It isn't, and what makes it worse is the fight over her estate. And it's not like she had a lot of money."

"Oh no. That sounds nasty. What's going on?"

"My brother Frank, before Genna passed, he got her to sign a new will that basically cut me out. I don't need the money, but it just burns me up."

Frank was a blowhard. "Did this happen close to when she died?"

"Oh yes, like a week or so. An aide told me about it, and when I asked Genna, she said she didn't want to fight anymore."

"Was your sister on pain meds?"

Marilyn nodded. "Yeah. She needed heavy doses to control the pain, and sometimes that wasn't enough. It was very difficult to see her suffer."

"I'm really sorry to hear that. If you don't mind me saying, you have a legal right to nullify the will she signed."

"What do you mean?"

"Being in pain and taking pain medication means your sister wasn't of sound mind to make such an important decision."

"He manipulated her."

"He might of, but either way it's not right, and you shouldn't allow it to stand."

"What can I do?"

"Let me call a good friend. He specializes in estate law. I'll make an appointment for you."

The feeling of discomfort Marilyn caused by wrapping her arms around me flooded back.

Wriggling my shoulders, the bad feeling receded. The call had to be from her brother, loudmouth Frank. The new will had been voided. Marilyn got her inheritance, and Frank was pissed at me.

15

WEARING A BASEBALL CAP OVER A BLOND, PONYTAILED WIG, I pulled open the door. There was a hint of Lysol in the air. The entire courtroom was standing as the judge lumbered to his chair.

No heads turned as I slipped into the back row. As people returned to their seats, I spotted the shiny black head of Nathan Royal. Sandwiched between a pair of blue-suited lawyers, Royal's light-gray suit made it doubtless who the defendant was.

Seated behind the prosecution was the woman Royal beat to the cusp of death. Shoulders pulled back like a marine, Cece Garner made me consider ditching my disguise as the clerk handed the judge a stack of papers.

Royal was like an old-time Mafia don: neither gave direct orders to anyone carrying out a crime. Filtering his wishes through several layers of associates was a big reason Royal avoided prosecution. Calling Royal slippery was akin to describing flowing volcanic lava as warm.

When working for Larson, I'd run into Royal. Larson warned me about him, but during a difficult assignment involving smuggled booze, Royal provided key information. He'd been helpful on another job, but as I inched closer to his inner circle, an uncomfortable feeling swelled to repulsion. When Royal wanted something, lines were not crossed, they were obliterated.

The first eye-opener happened a decade ago. Eddie Harris, a thug and enforcer for Royal's loan-sharking business, was arrested for breaking the leg of the son of a man past due on his debts.

It was an open-and-shut case that would result in Harris going away for at least ten years. Two weeks before Harris went on trial, the judge's ten-year-old son was scooped off the street into a van.

Speculation attributed it to someone the judge had presided over. A day before the trial was to begin, the kid was let go unharmed near Babcock Ranch. Royal's gang was suspected, but there was no evidence to make an arrest.

During the trial, the judge made several questionable rulings favoring Harris, and the teenager, whose leg was broken, backpedaled like an Olympian when identifying Harris as the aggressor. The case against Harris crumbled, and he was declared not guilty.

The brazen intimidation forced the county to increase the security for judges and their families.

Harris wasn't in the courtroom today, but Royal had filled two rows with his associates. An oversized thug sitting behind Royal stood, surveying those in attendance. The only thing sillier than this mountain—with a tattooed forehead, wearing an expensive suit—would have been if he wore a tutu.

Scanning the rear of the room, he stopped, looking directly at me. I held his gaze. His eyebrows arched. I didn't know this beast. Did he know me?

He sat and whispered to the man beside him. The judge cleared his throat, and the bailiff called the court into session.

The prosecutor said, "Your Honor, may I approach?"

"Yes."

Speaking in a hushed tone, the prosecutor handed the judge several documents. After reading them, the judge looked at Royal and his lawyers. "Mr. Temple, please approach the bench."

Royal's lawyer did as asked. Seconds later, he threw up his hands. The lawyer scurried back to his table with copies of the recant.

Royal shook his head as his lawyer informed him his alibi was being challenged. One of Royal's men leaned over the rail, asking Royal what was going on. The bailiff ordered him to sit as Royal said the witnesses were lying.

A wave of curses and vengeful promises brought a pounding of the gavel. "Order! Order, or I'll have you thrown out!"

The room quieted and the judge said, "We're going to interrupt the normal course of these proceedings, as a material issue has been brought to the court's attention."

Prosecutor Jenkins said, "The state calls Jeremiah Carlton to the stand."

The rear doors of the courtroom opened, and a guard escorted Carlton to the stand. The witness kept his head down as he made his way down the aisle. A cascade of hisses broke out as Carlton stepped into the well of the courtroom.

The gavel slammed. "This is your final warning!"

Duly sworn in, Carlton stared at his hands. Jenkins handed him a piece of paper. "Mr. Carlton, is this your statement?"

"Yeah."

"You understand that with this recant you have nullified your previous testimony regarding the whereabouts of Mr.

Royal on the night Cece Garner was viscously beaten. Is that true?"

"Yes."

"Tell the court where Mr. Royal was when Ms. Garner was assaulted."

"I don't know. I wasn't wit' him."

"Where were you?"

"Me and Sean, we was at my house."

"Was Mr. Royal there, with you?"

"No. I don't know where he was at."

"Why did you originally say you were with Mr. Royal?"

Carlton shrugged. "Royal said he needed a solid."

"Mr. Royal asked you to lie for him, in order to give him an alibi?"

"We go back a long ways . . . I was jus' tryin' to help out a brother."

"Are you going to change your testimony again?"

He shook his head. "Uh-uh. That's it, man."

"No further questions. Your witness."

Temple patted Royal's forearm before standing. "Mr. Carlton, you, and I might add, Mr. Brown, provided detailed and specific information in the testimony you gave a day ago on this very stand. How can you expect the jury to believe you now?"

"'Cause it's the truth, man."

"People say a lot of things they don't mean in exchange for something. Isn't that right, Mr. Carlton?"

"Objection."

"Sustained."

"Allow me to rephrase. Mr. Carlton, what were you offered in exchange for changing your story?"

Carlton looked at Jenkins, who nodded. "They got me out of a jam."

"What jam?"

"Well, we was picked up for dealin'."

"And the prosecutors agreed to drop the charges against you in exchange for your new testimony?"

"Yep, and they're getting me out of here."

"Out of here? What does that mean?"

"You know, the witness protection thing."

Temple smiled. "Is there anything else the state bribed you with?"

"Objection. The state will prove there was no bribery involved and that Mr. Carlton was offered protection in exchange for his testimony, as he fears for his life."

"Overruled. You'll have a chance to clarify on redirect. Continue, Mr. Temple, but be careful with your characterizations."

"Mr. Carlton, perjury is a crime. If I were you, I'd think long and hard about the deal you cut. Admit you changed your testimony to save yourself, and that your original testimony on the whereabouts of Mr. Royal was the truth. Are you ready to do that?"

He shook his head. "No."

"Why not?"

"Like I says, it's the truth."

Temple turned to the jury. "You can't trust someone like Mr. Carlton or his partner in crime, Mr. Brown. The two have long criminal records, and as the saying goes, they'd sell their mother to stay out of prison. Mr. Carlton changed his testimony in exchange for a deal—a sweet one, at that—with the state. I have no further questions, but I'm going to file a motion to have the latest version of Mr. Carlton and Mr. Brown's testimony thrown out."

Judge Wilkins said, "Considering the likelihood the testimony was prejudiced by the state's offer, the court is going to adjourn to give this testimony serious consideration. The court will recess for an hour."

Jenkins stood. "Your Honor, the state will show that Mr. Carlton's motivation was, in fact, pure, if it did involve a bit of prodding."

"Save it for your brief, Counselor." Wilkins pounded the gavel. "The court is in recess."

I sat stunned as Royal's henchmen slapped each other on the back. Royal was going to slip away. Again.

16

The bailiff bellowed, "Please rise for the Honorable Syd Wilkins."

Wilkins settled into his chair as those in attendance took their seats. He said, "I've decided to let these proceedings continue."

A rising murmur was quelled by a rap of the gavel. "Mr. Jenkins, call your next witness."

"The state calls Yakov Dubnik."

The courtroom doors opened, and a short man in a brown shirt and khakis was escorted to the stand. After he was sworn in, Jenkins asked him to spell his name and provide his address. Dubnik's East European accent came out as he answered.

"What do you do for a living, Mr. Dubnik?"

"I'm a mechanic for Home Tech. We fix appliances, like refrigerators."

"Please speak slowly, sir."

"Okay, okay."

"Mr. Dubnik, do you work any other jobs?"

"I drive for Uber and Lyft for extra money."

"And when do you drive for them?"

"Three nights a week: Monday, Wednesday, and Thursday."

"What times do you usually drive on those days?"

"Seven to midnight."

"Are there a lot of people to pick up during those hours?"

"Sometimes, but when it gets slow, I deliver food."

"Through the Uber app?"

"Yes, it's called Uber Eats. They don't pay much, but you get tips, most of the time."

"I'm interested in the food deliveries you made. Do you have a record of the deliveries from May 1, 2023?"

"Yes."

"Who produces the log?"

"Uber. It's in the report section, under earnings."

"And what does this report contain?"

"Um, what restaurant I picked up from, who it went to, and, uh, how much my share of the money was."

"And the day?"

"Oh yeah, I forgot; it has the day and the time also."

"Who generates this report?"

"Uber does."

Jenkins walked to the prosecution's table and picked up two sheets of paper. He dropped one on the defense table and approached the stand. "Mr. Dubnik, can you tell the court what this document is?"

"Yeah, it's the Uber log for May first."

"The log for what driver?"

"Oh, me. It has the pickups I did that night."

"Tell the court about the third food pickup you did, the night of May first."

He fingered the document. "Um, at 8:37 p.m., I picked up at Sushi Thai Too, on Airport Pulling Road, and took it to 312 104th Street."

"In Naples?"

"Yes."

"What time did you arrive at the 104th Street address?"

"Eight fifty-one p.m."

Jenkins turned to the jury. "The house Mr. Dubnik delivered to is rented by the same Mr. Carlton who testified earlier."

Temple got to his feet. "Objection. Just because food was delivered doesn't mean Mr. Carlton was there."

"Overruled."

Jenkins spun around. "Yes, that's true, a delivery, in and of itself, proves nothing." He picked up a remote off the defense's table. "However, as you'll see on the monitor, we can prove Mr. Carlton was there."

"Objection. We have no way to verify if this has been doctored."

Judge Wilkins said, "Overruled. It can be vetted later. I'll allow it. Please proceed, Mr. Jenkins."

"Mr. Dubnik, do you use a camera when you drive for Uber?"

"Yes. All the time. Naples is safe, but you never know who you are dealing with, and if you get in an accident, it can prove who was at fault."

"Thank you."

"Oh, and I save money on insurance too."

"That's good, and where is the camera?"

"I have two, one on the dash and one near my rearview mirror that covers the back seat and rear window."

"Thank you. Before playing this, let me remind the jury that this film runs from 8:49 p.m., when Mr. Dubnik pulled into the driveway for the home at 312 104th Street, and the clip ends at 8:52 p.m., when he backs out. Mr. Royal is accused of assaulting Ms. Garner on the same night at 8:45 p.m. at a location at least twenty, if not thirty minutes, away."

The monitor came to light and Jenkins hit play. Headlights

leading the way, the hood of a silver car pulled into a driveway. Jenkins paused the video. "Over the garage, the address of the home is visible. Let's continue."

The car stopped, and ten seconds later, Dubnik appeared, carrying two bags. He knocked on the door and it opened. The tape paused again. "Let me zoom in. You can see that it is, in fact, Mr. Carlton and the time is 8:50 p.m."

The tape slowly moved forward. Another man came into the picture, and Jenkins stopped it again. "That, ladies and gentlemen, is Mr. Brown."

He approached the stand. "Mr. Dubnik, can you tell us why both men came to the door?"

"The first guy didn't have any money for a tip, so the other man came and gave me a ten-dollar bill."

Jenkins smiled. "Very nice of him. Now, can you tell what they were doing in the house?"

"I'm not sure, but the TV, it looked like they were playing a video game."

"Let me play the rest of the tape."

Dubnik walked to his car, and a minute later, it backed away from the garage.

Jenkins said, "We'll play this again, and though the state may have offered to drop charges pending against Messrs. Brown and Carlton, this video documents, without a doubt, that they were not with Mr. Royal during the time the assault on Ms. Garner took place."

"Objection."

"Overruled."

Jenkins smiled. "Allow me to close by adding that in regard to the protective custody the state provided Messrs. Carlton and Brown, it was out of fear for their lives. They both insisted on it as a condition of finally telling the truth."

Seeing the noose tighten around Royal's neck should have

made me feel good. Instead, seeds of doubt crept in. Trying my best not to water them, I headed for the exit, reassuring myself I hadn't gone overboard trying to nail Royal.

Hands on the door, I heard what sounded like my name. I turned around. One of Royal's men had his forefinger pointed at me. His thumb was sticking straight up, mimicking a gun.

17

Walking past Yabba, I turned into Sugden Plaza. My back to Ocean Prime, I sat on the ledge and scanned the afternoon crowd. Kids surrounded a man twisting balloons into figures, generating a ten-dollar bill from a parent every two minutes.

Mario slid next to me. "This place is busy."

I whispered, "Who did you get the information from?"

"What are you talking about?"

I whispered, "Royal."

"I pieced it together myself."

"How?"

"By talking to a ton of contacts. I started hearing Carlton and Brown were hanging out with another guy, and I tracked him down."

"Who?"

"Troy Center. Carlton grew up with the guy."

"He works for Royal?"

"No. He's a mechanic at Tuffy's."

"He was at Carlton's house that night?"

"Yep. I asked him what they were doing, and when he said

they ordered from Sushi Thai Too, I tracked the driver down from the restaurant's CCTV footage."

"Who'd you tell?"

"Nobody."

I rolled my eyes.

"Honest. I didn't say anything."

Hissing, I said, "Royal knows it was us."

"Are you sure?"

"A thousand percent."

Mario scoffed, "He's going to be away for a long time."

"Maybe, but he's going to lash out at who put him there."

"Relax. He'll be behind bars. When is the sentencing?"

"You know how ignorant you sound?"

"What do you mean? I heard he's going to be put in Florida State Prison up in Jacksonville."

"Royal has a long reach."

"He's got more to worry about. Don't get paranoid."

"You're dead wrong. Royal's going to have time to ruminate over who put him there."

"All right already. What do you want to do?"

"I have an idea."

After outlining my plan, Mario said, "That'll probably work."

"I think so." I stood. "Let's get moving."

"Hang on a second."

"What?"

"Peterson said no problem with paying three hundred grand."

"Good."

"We should've asked for more. I told you he was loaded."

"Don't get greedy. Seneca said, 'It is not the man who has little that is poor, it is the man who desires more.'"

"Here we go again."

"It's true. Now, get on the Royal thing."

Dr. Bernie Schwartz had his office in the tall office building on the corner of Vanderbilt Beach Road and the Tamiami Trail. I entered the green-glass structure and checked the directory. It was filled with law firms and insurance companies.

The only medical office was Schwartz Podiatry. The sole person in his waiting room, a woman, was at the counter talking to the lady behind the desk.

As I signed in, the woman asked for an appointment on a Friday, and the lady responded that Dr. Schwartz only had office hours on Tuesdays. I didn't recall seeing that Schwartz had another office.

The woman booked her next visit and left. A minute later, I was ushered into a small exam room. Schwartz breezed into the room, extending his hand. "Mr. Beck, nice to meet you."

"Hello, Doctor."

"What's bothering you?"

"My foot. It hurts. Sometimes it's okay, but then all of a sudden, I get a sharp pain."

"Let's take a look." He motioned to the paper-covered exam table. "Sit, and take your shoe off."

I coughed while unlacing my shoe.

Pulling gloves on, he said, "Scoot back some."

The back of my throat tickled but I suppressed a cough.

He rolled over a stool and started probing. "Any pain?"

"No. Oh, there it is."

He ran a finger along the area before my toes. "Nothing visible from the outside. Let's take an X-ray. I'll be right back."

He pushed a cart into the room. "Stand on this." He clicked

twice and adjusted the machine over the top of my foot. "Hold still." Two more clicks.

"We'll see what's going on. Thank God X-rays are digital these days."

He looked at the screen. "When did this start bothering you?"

"About two weeks ago. When I got off the forklift, it was like, yowzer."

"This happened at work?"

"Yeah, that's when I first noticed it. Why? What is it?"

"It's difficult to pinpoint, but I'd say it's probably a stress fracture."

"You mean, like, a broken bone in my foot?"

"Yes, these types of fractures are hairline cracks in the bones of your foot."

"I can't believe it. And it doesn't show on the X-ray?"

"That's not unusual."

"Wow. Who'd of known?"

"Most people are unaware. But tell me, you get on and off the forklift a lot?"

I coughed, saying, "Sure, like fifty times a day."

"Sounds like a repetitive stress issue."

"Could be. I mean, I hop on and off a lot."

"We should test you for osteoporosis. It may be why you were susceptible to one."

"What can you do about it?"

"Well, these types of injuries heal themselves over time, provided you're not aggravating the issue."

"So, there is nothing I can do?"

"This is a work-related injury. I suggest you hold your employer responsible."

"I don't understand."

He opened a desk drawer and handed me a card. "This is a

lawyer I work with. He can help you recover any lost wages, plus a nice settlement to compensate for your pain and suffering."

"A lawyer?"

"Yes. He's right down the hall. I can get you in to see him immediately."

"But . . ." I had a small coughing fit. Schwartz dug in his pocket, offering me a lozenge. I'd rather take a brownie from Snoop Dog. "It's okay."

"We'll give you a prescription for crutches. I don't want you putting pressure on it. When you can, elevate the foot; it'll help reduce any swelling."

"But it's not swollen."

He opened the door. "Go see Mr. Stein and come back for another visit next Tuesday."

"Tuesdays don't work for me."

"I'm sorry, I only see patients once a week."

"Just once a week? Why?"

"Being an expert witness in court proceedings is the bulk of my practice these days."

After making an appointment I wouldn't keep, I headed for my car. Schwartz and the lawyers he worked with were no better than the pain clinics who handed out opioid prescriptions without any medical basis.

There wasn't a tinge of doubt that Dr. Schwartz had contrived a stress fracture to get Brett Caden off.

18

A STREAM OF CARS POURED INTO BONITA'S FLAMINGO ISLAND Flea Market. Squeezing my way between two huge planters, I exited onto a dirt access road. The pottery stall was so crowded with items, I wondered how anyone bought anything.

The sun was penetrating the baseball cap I was wearing. The main tent was busy. It was hard to determine who was shopping, browsing, or just looking for something to do.

The smell of cinnamon drew me to a table selling incense and candles. I felt a tap on my shoulder; it was Detective Moreno.

"Are you planning a seance?"

We walked down the aisle, past a booth selling mattresses. "I don't believe in that stuff."

"Me neither, but what do you think happens when we're dead?"

"I'm afraid nothing."

"No heaven or hell?"

"I think the best we can hope for is our spirit goes into something else or another universe."

"Got to be life out there somewhere."

"Probably is, but whether we go there after dying is up for debate, at best."

"Make the most of the time we got."

"Yep. Look, we need some help with Royal. I think he knows it was us who got the info to seal his conviction."

"What do you need?"

"A couple of unsubtle hints pointing to one or two of his guys."

"Misdirection, to make it look like an insider?"

I nodded. "There are two guys you want to tag with this: Rico Sanchez and Bobby Cash. They're both close to Carlton and Brown."

"I know them. They run the prostitution ring for Royal."

"Exactly. Pay them a couple of visits; make sure everybody sees you talking to them. We need it to look like they ratted on Royal."

"No problem. We can do that."

"I hope it'll throw him off our trail."

"It should."

"Yeah, if he doesn't have anyone feeding him info."

"In the sheriff's office?"

"Yeah."

"No way."

"Don't be so sure. Royal has been spreading money around for almost twenty years."

"I don't buy it."

"Oh yeah? Remember Cortez?"

"He was a one-off and a rookie."

"And that lady civilian up in admin?"

He put his hands on his hips.

I said, "Just trying to point out, Royal has bought a lot of souls."

"Yeah."

"Please don't tell anyone without a need to know, what you're doing."

We parted ways. I snaked through the stalls and turned on my heel. A figure in a straw hat ducked out of sight. I doubled back but couldn't see anyone. Spying a booth selling books, I went over, pretending to browse.

Reaching for a book on the left side of the table, another man came into view. He was looking right at me. He averted his eyes. I bought two paperbacks and headed for the parking lot.

I pulled onto Bonita Beach Road, and at the first light sent a text to Mario. Keeping my eyes on the rearview mirror, I headed west and made a left onto Tamiami Trail.

Traveling south for several miles, I turned into a shopping center and parked. I watched the entrance. Nothing appeared suspicious.

Mario's BMW pulled in. I got out and walked toward Five Guys.

We took our burgers to a table facing the entrance. I said, "I'm pretty sure I was being followed."

"What?"

I told him what happened at the flea market. He took a bite and dabbed his chin with a napkin. "You're paranoid."

"Look, I don't have to explain myself to nobody. Okay? I'm trying to tell you we need to be on the lookout."

"I am."

I scoffed, "You had your face glued to your phone, walking up here."

"Believe me, I'm on alert. But I gotta say, I don't think Royal's going to do shit. He's gotta be preoccupied, man. He's getting sentenced in two days."

"We should get out of town for a couple of days."

"I thought we both agreed, we're through running."

"It's not running; it's being prudent."

He took another bite, mumbling, "Call it what you like."

"I'm looking out for you, for both of us. When we stick together, it always works out."

"I know, bro. But Royal has got you paranoid."

"For good reason. You know what he's capable of."

"Killing isn't his style."

"But maiming is. I want to hold on to my cute looks."

He chuckled, "Is that what Karen called you? Cute?"

She did. "I don't know."

"You going to see her again?"

I wasn't. "Maybe."

"You should. She told Susan she really liked you."

"What are we, in elementary school?"

"Remember when you had the hots for Sabrina?"

She was the only sixth-grader with boobs. "Let's stay on track. I'm going to go up to St. Pete for a couple of days."

"Really?"

"You should come along. I mean, get your own place and all."

"We can share, like the old days."

"I'm getting claustrophobic just thinking about our old bedroom."

"Which one?"

I said, "The Mahoneys'. That was no bedroom; it was a frigging closet."

"Amen. How long were we there?"

"Two years."

"Small room or not, you can't compare it to being at Bryant's. What a fucked-up dude he was."

"You know, sometimes I wish he wasn't dead. I'd like to get back at that bastard."

Mario said, "We had a chance. But you said no. It would have been—"

"Are you getting out of town or not?"

"I have to think about it. Me and Susan are going paddle-boarding tomorrow."

"You can do that in St. Pete."

"We were supposed to go with another couple."

I stood. "Whatever. But don't say I didn't warn you."

He followed me out the door. "I get what you're saying, but my gut is telling me it's going to be okay."

"Relying on your gut is flat-out lazy. It's nothing but a guess, one influenced by emotion. You do the work, you don't have to rely on your gut."

19

A BLACK ESCALADE PULLED TO THE CURB. A COUPLE OF DOORS swung open. Three slabs of granite got out. One of the men knocked on the remaining door and Royal stepped out. Royal and his minions strode into the Cheetah's Lounge.

Two women in G-strings were gyrating on the stage. Royal and his men headed to the rear of the club.

One of his guys held the door open and Royal entered, saying, "Round up the boys. We got work to do."

"You wanna shut the club down?"

"No. What's the matter with you? We gotta carry on like everything is normal."

"Sorry, wasn't thinking."

"Don't think. I do the thinking around here."

"Who do you want me to get?"

"Pluck, Fat Man, Nino, and Griff."

"You got it."

Royal was seated in a high-back, red leather chair. In a semicircle were four men he'd known since middle school. Twirling his thumb ring, Royal said, "It's gonna get rough with me out of the picture for a while."

Pluck was as close to Royal as he let anyone get. "Don't worry, brother, we got the hold. Ain't nobody gonna step on your turf."

Royal nodded slowly. "I don't know how long it's gonna be, but I'll be back."

"We'll wait, man. And whatever you need when you're inside, you got."

Nino, who had a purple scar running down a cheek, said, "Damn right, whatever you want, I got it covered."

Royal clipped the end of a cigar. "I know you all got my back, but this is going to be different."

Fat Man, whose belly covered most of his thighs, said, "What are you talking about?"

Royal lit the cigar and took a puff. "I can't say. You'll know when you know. So, hang, and don't do nothing stupid. You hear?"

"Uh-huh."

"Pluck is in charge while I'm gone. I don't want no back talk or nothing. We gotta stay tight."

The men fist-bumped each other.

Royal said, "You take care of business, we'll stay on top, and you all will make serious money."

"We got it, boss. You don't have to worry."

"One thing you got to deal with is who snitched on me. I don't trust nobody outside this room. Some songbird has laid shit on my bed, and we gotta clip his motherfucking wings."

Nino said, "I feel your pain, brother."

"It's time we evened things up. Put the pressure on and flush out the motherfucker."

Fat Man said, "You know, one of the boys from Eighth Street, he said that cat, Mario, the one who works with Beck—"

Royal leaned forward. "What'd he say? That Beck turned on me?"

"Nothing like that, but he said that greasy-assed Mario was asking too many questions."

Talking for the first time, Griff said, "Me and Carlton, we're tight. If it was Mario who fucked us, he'll tell me."

Pluck said, "You right with that, Griff? Carlton ain't no talker."

Cracking his knuckles, Griff said, "You leave it to me; he'll be spouting like a fucking fire hose."

Pluck turned to Royal. "You done business with Beck. You think he turned?"

"No, but nothing surprises me. Nobody got any loyalty no more."

"If it was him, we'll find out and rip his fucking heart out."

Royal raised a hand. "If it's Beck, I want him alive."

"What are you talking about? If this bastard brought all this shit down on us, he needs to burn!"

"All in time. That cracker can be useful. He knows everybody up on high."

Pluck said, "The boss is right. Nobody gets done away with until Royal says so. You got that?"

"You sure about this, boss? It gets out we're cutting slack, the street will think we've gone soft."

Pluck said, "Then we show 'em we haven't."

Royal stood. "All right, boys. I'll see you when I see you."

The men began filing out, and Royal said, "Pluck, hang back."

Pluck closed the door. "You ain't got to worry; I'll keep them in line."

"They're going to get restless." Cigar in mouth, he paced the room. "You gotta be ruthless. Somebody wanders, smack 'em down, hard."

"They ain't gonna give me shit. These brothers are solid."

"Listen to me. People are gonna come after us. We can deal

with it, but if it comes from inside, we ain't gonna hold. So, keep your eyes open, even when you're sleeping."

"I got this."

Royal opened his arms, and the men hugged each other. "I know you do."

Breaking the embrace, Royal said, "Look, I'm gonna need you tomorrow."

"Sure, man. What's up?"

"I need you early. Meet me down at the marina, five in the morning."

"What? Five?"

"That's right, so, lay off the booze tonight. You gotta be sharp."

"No problem. That's damn early. What's going on?"

"You'll see in the morning, and be on time."

"Okay, no worries."

"Make sure you take the keys to your boat."

"Okay."

"Good. Now, go hunt down the scumbags who sold me out."

20

LARSON WAS STARING AT THE HORIZON WHEN I WALKED UP. "Hey, Ray."

"Beck, how are you?"

"Good. It's been a while since I've seen Vanderbilt Beach this quiet."

"Thank God. I really like it when the snowbirds start flying home."

"Traffic isn't such a problem anymore."

"Yeah, and you can get into restaurants."

"But without the part-timers, we wouldn't have all the places to eat that we do."

"Good point."

"You know I'm not a beach guy, but today, wow, it's a top tenner."

Larson said, "Sure is. Let's take a walk."

I ditched my flip-flops, and we headed to the shoreline.

We passed a couple of kids skid-surfing, and Larson pointed. "Look. There's a couple of manatees out there."

"Where?"

"To the left of the paddleboarder, about fifty yards further out."

"Yeah, I see them. They're some crazy-looking things. Like a hippo or something."

"They're actually related to elephants."

"Elephants?"

"Yeah, they use their lips like an elephant does with its trunk to pick up food."

"They just bob around in the water like a giant sea cow."

"It looks like that because they can't bend their necks, but they can swim twice as fast as an Olympic swimmer."

"What are you, a botanist?"

"Botanists study plants. You're thinking of a marine biologist."

"I can't believe I confused the words."

"It happens to the best of us."

"Look, I need to get as much as I can on Puzo."

Larson stopped walking. "You're going after him?"

"He's a turd, enabling other pieces of shit to abuse the system."

"No doubt, but he can be dangerous."

"More dangerous than Royal?"

"You win. Just be careful, okay?"

"What do you know?"

"First off, Puzo is a good lawyer. One of the best in Southwest Florida."

"I'm looking for dirt, not accolades."

"Just providing a rounded picture. Besides bending the rules, there's been a couple of rumors. Puzo likes to party, in a quiet way, but I've been told he likes to use cocaine when with the ladies."

"I never heard that. How good is that info?"

Larson raised his eyebrows. "Have I ever provided erroneous information?"

"Okay, okay."

"There was even one story, but I can't confirm all the details, where he was tipped off about a raid of a coke dealer he'd represented, and he went to the guy's house. As he was getting in his car to leave, the DEA pulled up."

"What happened?"

"They raided the place but didn't find anything. The lead agent believes Puzo snuck the drugs out."

"That's a dangerous move for someone like Puzo. Why would he do something like that?"

"It's not as risky as it seems. He would've claimed he was going to surrender the drugs along with his client in a bid to negotiate a better deal for the dope peddler."

"Pretty slick."

"And how. Puzo has been known to bend or break the rules. They just haven't caught him. Remember the Rudolph case?"

"Yeah, but besides that one, what others should I be looking at?"

"Remember the McKenzie trial? It was about the time you started working for us."

"The food truck guy whose wife was murdered?"

"That's it. The sheriff was sure McKenzie killed her, but his partner, who was a key witness, changed his story. He originally said he saw them arguing and that the last time he saw the wife alive, she was with McKenzie."

"Oh yeah. The partner disappeared right after testifying, right?"

"Yeah, and ten years later, almost to the day, he buys a big house on the beach in the Panhandle."

"He was paid off?"

"Maybe. Nothing but rumors at this point. They combed through both of their financial records, but nothing suspicious was found. But don't forget, Puzo was big on getting paid in cash."

"Cash. That's interesting."

"Puzo was screwed by a client. The guy had money, and it was frozen by the government. He gave Puzo a check, but they lost the case and the money backing the check was seized."

"Puzo got stiffed?"

"Yep, that's what led to his insisting on cash."

"That's something to look into. How about family?"

"Divorced, two kids who live with his ex."

"He lives in the Moorings?"

"No, Puzo is in Port Royal, but his house is being renovated."

"Damage from Hurricane Ian?"

"Hard to tell for sure. I heard it wasn't that bad, but Puzo fought with the insurance company and wrangled a big settlement from them. It's an older home, and he's doing a total renovation."

"Lawyers are ruining the homeowners' marketplace."

"No doubt. Too many inflated claims raise premiums for everybody."

I nodded. "They start on Puzo's remodel?"

"Yes. He's not living there."

"I'm sure it's a nice house."

"You know, I've never been there, but I've been told it has a big safe, encased in concrete, where he keeps his cash."

We did have something in common.

21

The moonlight reflected off the black water. Royal grabbed two gas cans out of his trunk and walked down the pier. He set them on the swimming ledge of his boat, *Royal's Flush*.

He hurried back to his car and slung a duffel bag over his shoulder. With his left hand he picked up a suitcase, and with his right, another can of gas.

Royal put the gas cans in the cockpit of his boat and the suitcase below deck. He opened the cabinet under the driving console, took his straw hat out, and sat in the captain's chair.

A pair of lights broke the darkness. Royal's gaze followed the headlights to a parking space next to his vehicle. It was Pluck, who made his way to Royal's boat and climbed aboard.

Eyeing the cans of gas, he said, "We going deep-sea fishing?"

Royal smiled. "You are, but I'm the catch."

"What are you talking about?"

"Get in your boat and follow me. And no running lights."

"You're freaking me out."

Royal backed up a few steps and beckoned Pluck, who

followed him. Royal lowered his voice. "You're my main man. You know that."

"No doubt, Royal. I'm with ya."

"There's no way I'm going inside. As much protection as we got, I'm the whale, and if anybody sticks a shiv in me, they're getting elevated and I'm a dead man."

"Nobody is gonna touch you."

"I can't take that chance."

"What's your plan?"

"Disappear for a while until I can figure things out. This shit came down too fast. I had it handled until . . . anyway, we got to get moving."

"Where to?"

"Follow me. And no lights."

Pluck stepped onto his boat, started the cabin-less Sea Ray, and watched Royal maneuver out of his slip. Pluck tossed his mooring lines onto the dock and pushed the throttle forward.

Royal surveyed the area as he traveled through the no-wake zone. Hitting Estero Bay, he sped up. He looked over his shoulder into the darkness. Pluck's craft was hard to see but was the only vessel in sight.

Pluck followed Royal into the Gulf of Mexico. Royal headed southwest. A mile offshore, he slowed down. He threw a bumper over the side and motioned for Pluck to sidle up.

As Pluck grabbed the side of Royal's boat, his gaze landed on the cans of gas. Before he could ask about them, Royal started undressing. Pluck said, "What's up?"

Royal unlocked the cabin door and headed under deck. "Tie up and come aboard."

Pulling on a new shirt from his suitcase, he popped his head up. "Get down here and help me."

Pluck stepped down. "Who the fuck is that?"

"A homeless guy. He's gonna be my double."

"Huh?"

"We're going to make it look like my boat exploded, and he's gonna be me. You are gonna have to go to O'Brien—and don't hand this off—you need to tell him he's gotta say the dental records match mine."

"Sly, man. That's super sly."

"When they find the boat, tell them you saw me go out alone, and say I wanted one last day on the water."

Pluck's smile crumpled. "But where you going to be hiding?"

"You'll know when you need to. I'll call when it's safe."

"But where am I taking you?"

"Marco Island."

"Marco's not a good place to hole up."

"I'm not staying."

"You should go to Mexico. You can disappear there."

Royal said, "I might. Come on. Help me carry him onto the deck and change his ass into my clothes."

They then climbed on board Pluck's craft. Royal knelt on the seating, and Pluck got behind the wheel. The nose of the boat lifted out of the water as Pluck pushed the throttle all the way down. Pluck held on to the rail. "Move it, man. It's gonna blow."

Pluck looked over his shoulder. "We're okay, man."

"Keep go—"

BOOM!

"Shit, there it goes."

BOOM!

"That's the second can. Let's get the hell out of here."

Four hours later, Royal stepped onto a desolate part of Lower Sugarloaf Key. Skirting Highway A1A, he walked a mile to the house he'd rented.

Royal closed the door to the modest home and swept the

dreadlocks wig off his head. He placed two burner phones he'd activated in Bonita on the nightstand, took his pants off, and unhooked the knee brace he wore to ensure a limp.

Royal flopped on the bed and flexed his leg. Reviewing the plan to lie low, monitoring developments before deciding his next move, he fell asleep.

22

Just three houses off the beach, the Airbnb, rented under Larson's name, was bigger than necessary. He was also a fan of eliminating surprises and may have wanted to project an image that I wasn't alone.

I gave Toby a treat, pocketed my cell and the burner for Mario, and headed out for a walk on the sand. A gentle breeze, sugar-white sand, and water that looked more like the Caribbean than the Gulf was the right medicine for my nerves.

Instead of ditching my flip-flops, I carried them, hoping to grab a bite to eat. There were a lot of people set up on the beach, but it wasn't crowded. I walked north, spying the sign for Woody's Waterfront.

Laura and I had been to a Woody's Waterside. Wondering if they had the same ownership, I checked my phone. She still hadn't reached out. I quickly dismissed the idea of calling her, telling myself I had to lie low. My stomach growled.

Not wanting any more reminders of a relationship on the rocks, I passed Woody's and headed for a place named the 82 Degrees Grill.

By the pool, a guitarist was strumming and singing a

country tune on top of a backing track. I took the stairs that led to a rooftop bar with amazing Gulf views. Whatever they served had to taste better up here.

My gaze went right to the St. Peter's Burger. At twenty-two dollars, it had better be Wagyu beef as advertised. Debating whether to forgo the bacon or the cheese, my burner phone vibrated.

Sticking up a finger at an approaching waitress, I hurried to a far corner and answered, "Hey, Mario."

"Where are you?"

"Up in St. Pete. You coming?"

"You can pack up and come back."

"I told you, I—"

"You're not going to believe it."

"What?"

"Royal's boat blew up. He was on it."

"What?"

My cell was ringing. As I dug it out, Mario said, "Royal's dead."

I said, "Hang on a sec. Larson's calling me on the other line." I told Larson I'd get back to him.

"That was Larson. He heard the news."

"Man, I can't believe it. What are the odds?"

"You know I don't gamble. Are you sure it was him?"

"Yep, he took his boat out this morning. A neighbor said they saw him leave in the dark, and a witness saw him at the marina."

"He was alone?"

"As far as I know."

"I don't know, it's too convenient. He was a day away from sentencing. It just feels . . ."

"It was his boat. I saw the name on the back of the boat on the news. How many guys have a boat named *Royal's Flush*?"

I looked at the screens over the bar: nothing but sports. “Let me get back to the house. I’ll call you later.”

Whether Royal was truly dead or not, I still had to eat. I ordered the burger to go.

Toting a shopping bag with my food, I left the restaurant and hit redial on my cell phone. “Sorry about that. I was on the phone with Mario.”

“He tell you about Royal?”

“Yeah, it seems surreal. I don’t know if I believe it. You think it’s him?”

“It sure looks like it. It was his boat for sure, and the coast guard recovered a body. It was badly burned, but I was told it matches Royal’s linebacker build.”

There weren’t many people Royal’s size. “When did this happen?”

“Somebody called it in around seven, off of Lover’s Key.”

“Any witnesses?”

“The park is still closed because of Ian, but a couple of boats in the area saw the smoke and came to see what was going on.”

“You think it was suicide?”

“That’s a hell of a way to go. And it’s not foolproof.”

“I know, but I’m just, you know, trying to figure this out.”

“We’ll have to see how his gang reacts, but I don’t think you’re going to have to worry about him.”

“I’m still staying for a couple of days.”

“Suit yourself, it’ll be a mini vacation.”

“What’s going to happen with the trial now?”

“They’ll postpone it, and once they get a death certificate, it’ll be marked as an abatement by death.”

“Royal gets off again, huh?”

Larson laughed. “I’m sure it wasn’t the way he would’ve planned it.”

"I'll call you later."

I tore the shopping bag open and opened the clamshell container. The burger was good. Not twenty-two dollars good, but it hit the spot.

Stuffing a fry in my mouth, I flipped open my laptop and logged on to my VPN. I typed "boat explosion in Lee County" into the search bar. A couple of videos populated the top of the screen. I clicked on the one from Fox 8 News.

Against a background of sand, a reporter said, "Early this morning, just off the coast of Lover's Key State Park, a boat exploded. Here's footage taken by our eyes in the sky."

The whooping sound of a helicopter blade was the soundtrack for an aerial view of a black plume of smoke rising from a boat.

"The coast guard responded to the blast, pulling the charred body of a male from the wreckage. The forty-two-foot boat was registered to a Nathan Royal of Bonita Springs, and he is believed to have perished in the accident. The boat was towed to a facility where a cause for the explosion will be sought."

I dialed Detective Moreno. "Hey, Mo."

"How are you, Beck?"

"You heard what happened to Royal?"

"Yep. Crazy, ain't it?"

"Can you make a few calls to your Lee County buddies and make sure it's him?"

He chuckled. "You've really built Royal up, haven't you?"

"Dotting the i's and crossing the t's."

"I don't think he's coming back from the dead."

"Let's see what the investigation reveals."

"They've got a good marine unit in Lee."

"Are there any Lee County guys on the Royal gravy train?"

"If it was common knowledge a cop was on the take, they'd be long gone."

"I know, but what about any rumors?"

"Hold on, Beck. You and me, we would've known, right? I don't get where all this anxiety is coming from."

"My gut." I regretted saying it was nothing solid, but that's what it was. "It just feels off. You know, the timing, and he was alone."

"Hey, who knows? Royal was out there with extra gas cans, maybe he was planning to cross the Gulf into Mexico."

"Maybe. He was into being on the water, but Mexico seems like a stretch."

"Yeah? Remember that case in Lee County, that sleazebag Slaton? He was hiding out in Mexico for twenty-seven years until they caught him last year."

I did. "All right already. Just keep an eye on it, okay?"

23

Jumping on to my VPN, I clicked open Google Earth, navigating to Florida's Panhandle. It was amazing, all kinds of information was a click away. About a year ago, I'd seen a car with the Google logo, driving around with a camera on its roof. But that was it. Were they using satellites to capture what everything looked like?

There were miles and miles of shoreline. Beautiful golden beaches. What way was there to nail Puzo? Getting him disbarred was the goal. Finding support that Puzo had paid a witness to change his testimony would go a long way.

The grassy, raised berms of Inlet Beach reminded me of the beaches in South Carolina. Zeroing in, there it was, the home owned by Bill McKenzie, the food truck man accused of murdering his wife. Sitting on stilts, it was a football field away from the gleaming Gulf of Mexico.

The two-story house was grayed by the elements. The sun and salt made everything look older, including people.

Though built in 1980, it was new to McKenzie. The tax records said he'd bought it two years ago, paying half a million for the home.

You couldn't trust the numbers in the system; there could have been an error, or more likely, with Puzo's money, he could have supplemented the purchase with a suitcase of cash.

Reviewing the modest home and those around it, the five hundred thousand McKenzie paid fit the value of other transactions at the time.

A half a million to be on the beach seemed like a steal, especially compared to South Florida. Unless you were looking for a parking spot, you couldn't get near saltwater in Miami or Naples for that sum.

McKenzie, who had never remarried, was driving a five-year-old car and ate at Denny's. If Puzo had given him a pile of dough to change his testimony, McKenzie had monk-like restraint.

Closing the browser, I sat back and closed my eyes. Puzo's insistence on getting paid in cash had made him more secure, but had it created a vulnerability?

Hitting his stockpile of money wasn't ideal. Getting him disbarred was more devastating; he'd lose his livelihood and get disgraced in the process. Or was it? If Puzo had enough money squirreled away, the loss of income would be meaningless.

If I couldn't uncover a scandal that disbarred him, the focus would shift to his stash of cash. Taking out a burner phone, I called Mario.

"Hey, what's up, Beck?"

"Puzo. He's remodeling his Port Royal house."

"Okay, what's the tie-in?"

"Check into who's doing the work. See if we can get a subcontractor to hire one of us."

"You want to get inside?"

"Exactly."

"That shouldn't be too hard. Every contractor is looking for workers."

"Let me know."

"I'll get you in tomorrow. Guaranteed."

I palmed my regular cell and put in the passcode. No messages. Laura was stubborn. Mom used to call Dad stubborn. It was a good-natured ribbing that he'd respond to by saying, "If you don't stand for something, you'll fall for anything."

It was a tough concept to understand at the age of eight, but he took the time to explain it to me. It would be the way I'd teach my kids, if I ever had any. I wouldn't belittle them like Bryant had done.

Being called an idiot still stung, especially the time when Bryant said—in front of the kids in the neighborhood—that I was stupider than a doorknob. He grabbed my arm, lifting me off the ground, because I had put a can of coffee in the refrigerator like my mom used to do.

It was impossible to understand at the time, but Bryant was covering his shortcomings by harping on the smallest mistakes by others. The humiliation he regularly heaped on Mario, Bev, and me had a lasting impact. It was just below the surface, and talking about it was the last thing I wanted to do.

How do you explain you were more like a slave than a family member? Bryant had us doing all kinds of chores. Dirty, disgusting chores like unclogging a toilet with our hands, having to gut the fish he caught, and other things we didn't have the know-how to do and were still berated for. None of the foster fathers were like Dad, but Bryant was a monster.

Losing both parents made counseling automatic. Social services may have been well-meaning. Maybe they had too many cases, but trying to communicate that there was a problem in the foster home was impossible. "Give it more time" was the mantra. Mario and I got away, but poor Bev was left behind.

A proper system, especially one to protect children, would

never allow someone like Bryant to have custody of a child. The frustration and pain he caused had generated my first thoughts of getting revenge.

The idea of evening the score grew after Mario and I escaped from Bryant's tyranny. After stints as dishwashers at a diner in Philly, a server told us about a fish-processing plant on Delaware Bay. The money was better, and after two months, the preoccupation with survival receded, but as it turned out, not for long.

The twenty-year-old Ford Focus we bought by scraping together eight hundred dollars brought us a level of mobility. The first trip we took was a weekend getaway to Assateague Island, a barrier island off the coasts of Maryland and Virginia.

We pitched our tent and went to explore the remote parts of the island. A pack of wild horses held our attention until I spotted a lone fisherman. He was perched on a narrow strip of land elevated above the water.

It was the sighting that blossomed into an obsession. There was a way to kill Bryant and have it look like an accident.

Monday morning, the foreman at the fish plant, Mallory, seemed to have it in for me. He had been giving me shit for weeks. He watched as a couple of workers asked us about our weekend. Five minutes before starting time, he barked at us to get to work.

I took my position on the line, and Mallory stood behind me. He was yelling at me and began poking me with his frigging stick. It wasn't hard to see this wouldn't end well. But I never imagined we'd be back on the run, and I'd become known by my middle name.

24

I pulled into Moorings Beach Park. It was private property, but at night no one monitored the parking lot. "Come on, Toby. Let's go for a walk."

It might have been being by the water or the extra-long leash I used at night, but Toby romped around as if he had the key to the snack drawer. We walked toward Doctor's Pass. You could hear the water lapping against the shoreline. I looked out. No boats, but there was a man at the end of the jetty.

The leash jerked. I'd stopped in my tracks. "Sorry, boy. Let's go home."

Toby wasn't having it. He pulled me along as I tried to push away the memory of trying to kill Bryant.

The stoics said regret was when past events consumed our present life. It made sense, but that didn't make it easy. My cell rang. It was Mario.

"Hey, what are you doing?"

"Walking Toby. What's going on?"

"Just confirming everything is set for tomorrow. I'll text you the address."

"Thanks."

The truck bounced up Puzo's driveway. Even the pavers were being replaced. The driver backed up to a three-car garage and shut the engine. He grabbed a clipboard off the dash and said, "The others just pulled up. Grab a couple of guys and unload the cabinets into the garage. Remember, keep the product separate. Most of it's for the kitchen, but there's a number of units for the bathrooms, bar, and built-ins."

We hopped out, and he unlocked the rear doors. I said, "We should probably stage the upper baths by bringing them upstairs. It'll make it easier on the installers."

"You want to hump it up, go for it. As long as the site foreman signs for the load, I'm good."

Two of us picked up a long crate and headed for the garage. Setting the box down, another pair of laborers came in with more cabinetry. I said, "Hey, how's it going?"

"All right. You new?"

"Yep. Just started."

"Man, it's a hot one today."

"Yep. They said we're going to bring some of this upstairs."

"That's bullshit. The installers handle that."

"I'm only telling you what the man said. After we bring in a couple more, I'll go inside and check it out. There's a lot of guys working this job; maybe we can tell them we'd be in the way."

"Good idea."

On his phone, the driver sat in the air-conditioned cab while we unloaded the truck. I slipped into the house. A pair of electricians were on ladders installing LED lights. The new white oak floors were covered with runners. My gaze settled on a curving staircase with iron railings.

Taking the stairs two at a time, I hit the landing in seconds.

Not only could you see most of the main area, but you had a view of the water out back. As a boat motored past, my thoughts went to Royal and the explosion. A hammering sound brought me back, and I headed for a pair of double doors.

It led to the master, the likely place to put a safe. Two men were laying tile in the master bath. I walked into the closet. It was larger than any of the bedrooms I'd slept in as a kid. The flooring was intact. I knocked along the walls. No dummy walls.

The second closet was smaller. There was no place for a safe. I hustled down the hall into another bedroom and came up empty. There were two more rooms on the floor.

The next bedroom had a view of the driveway. I went into the closet. There it was, the shiny door to the safe. It had an electronic pad. The safe was a Barska and new. Touching the pad, it came alive, flashing red.

My shoulders sank. It was a biometric safe. The new generation of safes were difficult to break into. Could it be hacked somehow? I jumped.

"What are you doing?"

"Oh, just looking. We're staging the cabinetry, and I_was thinking we could load some in this closet."

He was one of the masons. "You try and open that?"

"No. Of course not."

He smiled. "Get on your way. And don't put anything in here."

"Sure"—I pointed—"the master closet makes more sense."

Taking the stairs, it was clear I'd have to get sweaty and haul a bunch more boxes until I could fake an illness and call for an Uber.

25

WATCHING THE NEWS WAS SOMETHING I AVOIDED. YOU WERE nothing but a zoo animal being fed what they decided to give you. But the way the people in my circle lapped up the Royal story had me channel surfing.

Pictures of the blackened boat were all over the TV and web. Within hours, the press had connected the dots and ran the story as a suicide to avoid a certain twenty-year prison term.

Royal was thirty-eight. If he had been able to avoid getting stabbed with a shiv behind bars, he'd be close to sixty when released. Suicide was a convincing alternative, but why not swallow a handful of pills?

Instead, Royal fleeing before sentencing made more sense. How much gas would you need to cross the Gulf of Mexico? I started Googling maps of the area. Had he been trying to head north, into Alabama? I was pretty sure he had family in the Cotton State.

A strip of land, known as Isla Mujeres, was just off the coast of Cancun. At three hundred and fifty miles, it was the shortest distance to Mexico and away from American justice. Answers on how long it would take were all over the place, but no matter what, it was a doable trip in the right boat. And Royal's was the right one.

I studied images of Royal's vessel being towed by the coast guard. Something caught my eye. It looked like a red gas can. I zoomed in. It was.

I sat back. Royal had blown himself up trying to flee. How? The gangster liked cigars. Had a celebratory smoke been his downfall? It'd feel good to have something to confirm he was gone.

Pulling my burner out, I called Mario. It went to voice mail. I left a message and took the dog for a walk. As Toby was doing his business, a red Ferrari motored by, revving his engine to make sure everyone saw him.

Scooping up what Toby left, my mind shifted to Caden. The bones of the plan were in place. The Royal distraction had receded, and it was time to flesh out what was to be done about Caden.

I unleashed Toby, gave him a Milk-Bone, and dialed Larson. "Hey, where are you?"

"At the beach. What's up? You have something more on Royal?"

"No. But I'm thinking he may have been on the run when the boat blew."

"It's likely. He had extra gas cans aboard. He may have been running to Mexico."

"Maybe, but I think it might have been the Bahamas. It's under a three-hundred-mile trip."

"That's less than Cancun."

"Exactly, and from the Bahamas he could move around to different islands, all with separate law enforcement and government agencies."

"Good point."

"And if he made it to the Dominican Republic, they don't have an extradition treaty with the US."

"Really?"

"Yes, I'm surprised you didn't know that."

Larson said, "At eighty-seven, Michelangelo said he was still learning. If that's good enough for him, it's good enough for me."

"He was something. You ever read his biography?"

"Yeah, a couple of years ago. I don't think there's ever been another one like him."

I said, "Possibly Elon Musk."

"Maybe. He's got forty years to catch up."

"They're both interested in a wide range of subjects."

"I wonder if Musk pursues any kind of artistic expression."

I'd read that he drew. "I think he sketches."

"Cool."

"Look, I need a favor."

"Sure. What's up?"

"I have to borrow your Ferrari."

Larson hesitated. "What for?"

"I need to get close to Caden."

"What do you want to do, impress him?"

"Not really. He's a car buff, and it might be the way in."

Larson exhaled heavily. "All right, but promise me you'll be careful with her."

I laughed. "It's a she?"

"Promise me."

"Don't worry, I'm hardly going to drive it."

"I've had it two years, and nobody else has ever driven it."

"Thanks, buddy."

"It's not quid pro quo, but this seems like a good time to ask you for a favor."

"Uh-oh, here it comes."

"It's nothing big, and she is willing to pay."

"Who are you talking about?"

Larson gave me a quick briefing, and I said, "Okay, I'll talk to her. Give me her contact info."

I jotted it down and said, "I'll be back in town soon. I'll see her, then swing by and pick the car up."

Circling the parking lot for Galleria Shoppes at Vanderbilt, I regretted promising Larson I'd meet the woman with an issue.

Saturday mornings they hold a farmers' market, providing good cover. There were more people than I'd figured. Had the overcast sky driven people to find other activities?

I parked by Angelic Desserts and walked toward a sea of white tents. Anna Barone was in her late sixties. Short and gray haired, she was wearing a dark blue dress and flats.

I sidled up to her. "Anna?"

"Yes. Mr. Beck?"

"Let's walk. You have breakfast yet?"

She had a limp. "Yes, I have a grapefruit every morning, but I can go for a cup of coffee."

"How about Poached? We can grab a table outside."

"Perfect."

I grabbed two coffees and we sat. "Tell me what's going on."

She frowned. "Well, all my life I've been active and did my best to stay as fit as possible."

"You've succeeded."

She scoffed, "Not since my hip replacement."

"It set you back?"

"Not the actual surgery, but this." She stuck her foot out. "The surgeon screwed up, leaving me with drop foot."

"Did you pursue a malpractice claim?"

"Even though I don't need the money, I did. But the judge dismissed the case."

I knew but asked anyway. "What do you want?"

Barone set her coffee down and leaned in, hissing, "To get even."

26

Toby jumped off the bed, waking me. The fact that he was wee-wee pad trained wasn't what kept me in bed. I cleared my mind and brought up William Puzo. He needed to pay for his role in the Caden-Peterson disaster.

The question was how. The easy answer was throwing a hurt on him, but organized crime tactics were simplistic, effective in getting temporary satisfaction, but without pleasure. It wasn't what I was after.

Shoving out of my head the thought of putting the sleazy lawyer in a hospital bed, I let ideas float in and out. It was a weird way to brainstorm—technically, brain-drizzling.

The money angle kept leaking in. Was there a safecracker who knew the work-around for a biometric lock? Despite making inquiries, none had surfaced. Yet.

Puzo took risks defending his clients. But where he was concerned, he'd been as careful as a brain surgeon. There had to be something—something that could lead to his disbarment.

As the sound of Toby's paws on the tile grew nearer, an idea came to mind. I needed to think it through. It was dangerous, carrying the risk I'd land behind bars for a decade or more, but it made me smile.

Swinging my legs off the bed, I said, "Come on, boy. Let's get you some breakfast."

The sky to the east lit up as Toby licked his bowl clean. I thought the Puzo plan through. There was a chance it could blow up on me, but I'd checked all the boxes.

I savored my second cup of coffee while running through the idea again. It was a go. I filled Toby's bowl with water and left the house. There was something important to do before tackling Puzo.

Dr. Schwartz normally left his house at seven each morning. Sometimes he'd make a detour before arriving at his office by nine, and other times he'd be behind his desk at eight.

According to Google, podiatrists in Naples earned over two hundred thousand a year. Schwartz's home in Pine Ridge Estates was worth six million. As attorneys knew, ripping off insurance companies was the path to riches, but this house was in his wife's name. Her father was a big-time developer.

One of the four garage doors lifted. The taillights of a BMX X7 lit up. It was 7:01 a.m. Schwartz was corrupt but punctual.

It was a short ride to his office. He parked, and I backed into a space with a line of sight to his Beemer. Once the clock hit 8:45 a.m., I got out of my car.

If Schwartz was going anywhere, it would be for lunch. I got out, stretched, and circled the parking lot twenty times.

At 11:59 a.m., Schwartz walked into the lot, got in his BMW, and pulled out. I followed him. He made a quick stop at ABC Liquors on Immokalee Road and came out with a bottle of wine.

I stayed a quarter of a mile behind Dr. Schwartz as he drove north on Route 41. As we passed Bonita Beach Road, I looked left. It was perfect; dark clouds were gathering.

We continued into Estero, and at Coconut Road the podiatrist made a right. I smiled, thinking I'd gotten him easier than anticipated. Schwartz headed deep into the parking lot for Marriott's TownePlace Suites and pulled into a space.

Holding the bottle he'd bought, Schwartz just about skipped to the hotel's entrance. I took a couple of photos for good measure and followed him as he went in and registered.

I pretended to be talking on my phone and hovered near a sitting area by the front desk. As the clerk handed Schwartz back his driver's license, I shuffled closer.

"Here are your keys, Mr. Schwartz. Room 214. The elevators are to your left."

"Thank you."

The podiatrist made a quick call while waiting for the elevator, saying, "See you in five," as he hung up.

Schwartz stepped into the elevator, and I kept my eyes on the entrance. A woman in painted-on white jeans came in. As she surveyed the lobby, I took the stairs to the second floor.

I came out of the stairwell as the elevator dinged. Ducking into the ice machine alcove, I took my phone out. Ms. White Jeans checked the direction of the room numbers and went straight to number 214.

Clicking the video button, I filmed her as she straightened her blouse and stuck her chest out. She knocked on the door, whispering, "Guess who?"

The door opened. Smiling like a teenager on the last day of school, Schwartz embraced the woman. Shirtless, Schwartz put his hands on the lady's ass. I couldn't have planned it any better.

I waited until they went inside, then I shuffled down the

stairs. His wife wasn't paying me, but there was no doubt Schwartz would regret his afternoon delight.

Pulling out of the hotel's parking lot, large drops of rain hit the windshield. It was raining on Schwartz's parade.

27

Lock Up Self Storage didn't have a perimeter fence. Puzo had two storage units at the Pine Ridge facility. The lack of a fence was one less thing to deal with.

Mario and I parked a block away, but we had a clear sight line of the building. We sat quietly. Fifteen minutes went by without us seeing a car or person.

I said, "Straighten your mustache, it's off a little."

He pulled the sun visor down and adjusted his Fu Manchu. "I can't believe this was a thing back in the day."

I patted my wig. "It suits you."

We put baseball caps on and surveyed the area. It was cemetery-like. "Let's get moving."

We took two purse-sized packages out of the trunk and walked to one of the zillion places people paid to hold things they should have thrown out.

"It's hard to believe the number of these storage facilities. It's like they're self-propagating."

"Fifteen years ago, you couldn't find one."

"We've become a country of hoarders."

A motion-sensing light clicked on.

"Keep your head down. Building three is to the left."

We scurried to the side of a building and waited until the light went off. Hugging the wall, we made our way to one of Puzo's units.

I said, "This is the larger one."

Mario replied, "Okay. Let me at it."

He took out a ring of keys, paged through them, and found the master key he wanted. He stuck it in the lock, and it popped open. "Easy peasy, man."

Mario bent down and was about to grab the handle. I said, "Go slow. These roller doors are loud as hell."

"Is hell really loud?"

"Open it halfway."

He rolled the door up halfway. We snuck underneath and lowered it. Eyes adjusting to the darkness, we clicked on our flashlights. The unit was filled with blanket-covered furniture and boxes. I shined my beam on a long, blanket-covered piece. "That looks like it might be a dresser."

"It does."

"We have to be careful. I want it put back just the way it was."

"Don't worry, you forget I worked for Allied one summer?"

I hadn't forgotten anything in my past. "We need access to one drawer—that's it. Don't rip any more tape off than necessary."

Mario took out a box cutter. "We got a whole roll."

He slit the tape in two places and shimmied the blanket up. I said, "That's good. Pull it up a smidgen more and hold it."

Mario held it, and I dumped two packages into a drawer. He pulled the blanket down, and Mario taped it back up. "Looks good, no?"

I put the beam of light where he'd doctored the packing. "Perfect. Let's go."

It was a form of ticking time bomb. The timeline was longer than twenty-four hours, and when it went off, though there wouldn't be an explosion, it would still be destructive.

28

Admiring the silver sports car from the steps to Caden's house, I hit the bell. Caden pulled his head back when he saw me. "You're the guy, we spoke to, uh, the other day."

"Yes. I'm Beck."

"Right."

"I'm sorry to bother you, but"—I turned toward the driveway—"look what I got."

"A Portofino. It's always been one of my favorite Ferraris. I love the way it drives. It's like it's nailed to the road."

"It's just another world."

"I told you."

"I know, after I left here that day, I couldn't get the idea of getting one out of my head. I mean, you made such an impression on me."

He started down the stairs. "I knew you'd like it. You gotta be a dick not to."

"You were on the money."

"That's a 2020."

"Wow. How did you know?"

He pulled open the driver's door. "I've been buying these cars for years."

As he climbed in, he said, "I love the color. Ferrari's silver is unlike anybody else's. Not even Lambo has paint like this. Look at the way it goes with the interior: it's perfect."

"It is pretty."

"Where'd you get it?"

"A buddy of mine in Sarasota owned it, and he was looking to upgrade."

"It's only got twenty-three hundred miles on it. This baby is brand new."

"I know."

"It's the most drivable Ferrari they make. You can use it every day."

"You want to take it for a spin?"

"Nah, I had one of these when I first got into Ferraris. Come on. Let me show you my collection."

"I'd love to see them."

Caden tapped on the garage keypad. As the double garage door lifted, a flood of cold air hit us. A white Maserati was parked next to a red Ferrari in the triple-deep cavern he called a garage. The gleam on the resin floor screamed hospital.

There was room for six cars plus. "Wow. I can't believe it." I pointed to an off-white car. "What model is this? It looks a little like mine."

"That's an F8 Spider. It's got seven hundred and ten horsepower. Yours is just six hundred."

"Wow, that's a big difference."

Caden grabbed a cloth and polished the fender. "It is. Top speed is two hundred and eleven."

"That's not a car, it's a frigging rocket ship."

Caden smiled. "My Aventador blows it away. It's got seven

hundred and forty horse and tops out at two hundred and seventeen miles an hour."

"That's crazy."

"You think that's fast? See the red one? It's my Ferrari LaFerrari Aperta."

"I never heard of that model."

"They only made two hundred and ten of them."

"That's nothing."

"And it's got nine hundred and fifty horsepower."

"That's crazy. You can't use all of that."

"Sometimes the Lamborghini dealer in Broward County arranges to use the Homestead Speedway, and we run the cars there."

"On a track? You race them?"

"Sure. It's a lot of fun."

"You have to know what you're doing to go that fast."

"I've been running cars since I was a teenager. Check out this one." Caden approached a yellow angular work of art. "Lambo brought back the Countach."

"I heard about that model."

"They only made a hundred and twelve of them."

"That's rare. It's probably a good investment."

"It is. But it wasn't cheap."

"What Ferrari is this one?"

He pulled open the car's door. "A GTS 788. It's the successor to the 488 GTS."

I inhaled. "I love the smell of leather."

"Nothing beats Italian leather, especially from Poltrona Frau."

I touched the dash. "Beautiful feel, and the stitching is gorgeous."

"It's all done by hand."

"I guess you'll never drive an SUV."

He scoffed, "I had one a while ago, but never again."

He had to be referring to the one he slammed into Peterson's wife. "I can see why. How do you choose what to drive?"

"I kind of rotate them, but I don't drive the Countach much. I want to keep the mileage super low."

"Good strategy to keep the value high."

"I know the market for high-end cars better than the people who work in the industry."

Was he going to injure himself by patting himself on the back? "I'm sure you do. I guess this is your main hobby?"

"I'm also a five-point-five tennis player. I could be a teaching pro, but there's no money in that."

"That's sounds like a professional."

"I could've been one, but as a kid I wanted to party, not play ten hours of tennis a day."

"It's a grind."

"It sure is."

I swept my hand. "It looks like you made a damn good decision doing whatever you do."

"I could've kept going, but how much do you really need?"

I shoved, *Yeah, you only get one inheritance* back in my mouth. "Marcus Aurelius said, 'The only wealth you own forever is the wealth you have given away.'"

He looked at me as if I'd asked him the meaning of life. "Yeah, whatever. For me, I just said to myself, I got more money than I know what to do with, and now is the time to party, you know?"

"Exactly."

"Hey, I got to run. I'm meeting a couple of buddies for cocktails."

"What car are you taking?"

"The Maserati. I try not to drive my babies when I'm throwing back a few."

"Good move." I lowered my voice. "I like to do a little snow, every now and then. I should keep that in mind."

"Coke doesn't affect the way you drive like booze does."

"Really?"

"Trust me, I know all about it."

"Okay. Say, one of my friends, he's also into cars, he puts together rallies. It'd be good to have you participate. We take a drive and then grab dinner."

"Sounds good, I'm always up for meeting new people. Let me know."

Caden was on the hook. It was a start. A good one. But driving along Vanderbilt Drive, I knew reeling in someone like him was going to be tricky. The plan would have to be executed with the precision of a space exploration mission.

29

Toby tugged the leash as we walked into the Bonita Beach Dog Park. Hurricane Ian had shifted things, and now you had to walk through water at the entrance.

His tail was wagging like a metronome on speed. As he lifted a leg to drop his scent, my phone vibrated. It was Detective Moreno. "Hang on a sec, Mo."

I unclipped Toby's leash, and he bounded toward a handful of dogs splashing in the water. "Hey, sorry about that. What's going on?"

"A cop buddy of mine in Lee just told me they matched the body found on the boat. It's Royal."

"How did they do the ID?"

"Dental records."

"It just doesn't make sense."

"It's him, Beck. Royal is toast." He laughed. "You like that pun?"

"Funny. Did they say how it exploded?"

"They think it was a cigar. The marine unit found gas on the deck."

"Royal smoked cigars, but I figured he was smarter than that."

"He might have been street-smart, but he sure as hell wasn't a genius."

"It's crazy he was so careless."

"Don't forget, he was on the run and probably rushing."

"They find any money on the boat?"

"Not that I know of."

"Check and let me know."

"All right. Have a good one."

"You too."

I kicked off my flip-flops and walked into the water. Ankle deep, I reached into my cargo shorts and pulled out an orange ball. "Toby! Toby! Go fetch!"

I tossed the ball, and he took off in the direction of it.

He was as carefree as it got. Was it possible for a human to get there? The thought of being completely worry-free scared me. It was easier imagining me walking around on Mars. Being hypervigilant was impacting my life. Was there a compromise to be had?

I made a call. "Laura, how are you doing?"

"Okay."

"What's the matter?"

"I called you three days ago."

Schwartz and Puzo had distracted me. "Oh, yeah. I was so tied up with work; it's been a crazy week."

"It only takes five minutes to return a call."

"You're right. I'm really sorry. It's been so busy."

"You have to decide what's more important to you: work or a relationship."

"It's not cut-and-dried. I'm trying to figure things out."

"Call me when you do. I have to go."

Click.

What the heck? Okay, a couple of days passed, but we weren't dating anymore. And she was easygoing?

"Toby! Come here, boy!"

His ears went up. I waved the ball and threw it a couple of car lengths from where he was. He galloped after it.

After a dozen more tosses, I called Mario to let him know about Royal, and we headed home.

With Larson's Ferrari in my garage, I parked my car in the driveway and put Toby on his leash. I hosed him off and towel-dried him before going inside. As he devoured his food, I made a call and left the house.

The rehab section of Collier Sports Medicine took up the ground floor of a building on Medical Drive. Two men with crutches waited for the elevator. I took the stairs, hoping the receptionist wasn't the girl I briefly dated.

A gray-haired woman told me to wait. The walls were lined with sports jerseys of the players who were patients. People trusted doctors who worked on athletes but missed the fact that the outcomes were good because the patients were young and fit.

A side door opened, and Dr. Russo waved me in. "I only have a couple of minutes."

"That's all I need."

We retreated to his office. A pair of signed footballs sat on the credenza. "Those new?"

"No." He slid a cabinet door open, revealing a mess of memorabilia. "If a patient gives me something, I try to display it when they come in."

"They teach you that in med school or business school?"

"My dad always told me, the customer is king, even if you're a surgeon."

"Smart man."

"He truly was. What did you need?"

"I'd like to get up to speed on drop foot and hip replacements."

"Are you referring to the possible causation of drop foot in patients that undergo a hip replacement?"

"Yes."

"It's a fairly common presentation in hip arthroplasty, but most patients recover full use."

"What causes it?"

"A compression of a nerve, the peroneal nerve, in the leg. That nerve controls the muscles involved in lifting the foot."

"How often does it happen?"

"Well, broadly speaking, from one to four percent of patients. Of course, it depends on the patient. Those with previous hip surgeries and those with developmental hip dysplasia are more susceptible to problems."

"Dysplasia?"

"Some people are born with underdeveloped hip joints."

"Excluding those cases, is it the surgeon that causes it?"

Russo shifted in his chair. "These surgeries are commonplace, but let's not forget they're still complicated."

"I get it, but is it surgical error?"

"It could be. What details can you share?"

"I'm still collecting information, but this lady got a new hip over a year ago and still has foot drop."

"Females have a higher problem rate—"

I laughed. "Is that in general?"

He smiled. "I was referring to the incident rate of drop foot."

"Just kidding, Doc."

He nodded. "Of course, you raise all kinds of risk levels, in any surgery, if it is performed by a junior surgeon."

"Experience counts."

"Undoubtedly. You can risk inexperience with a new hair-stylist but not with surgery."

The surgeon Barrone used was well-regarded, with twenty years of experience. "Thanks for your time, Doc."

"Anytime, Beck. And thanks for the donation. It's going to go a long way for the kids at the Guadalupe Center."

"Happy to help. I'm also gonna come up with something for you to auction off at the charity event."

"Thank you. Why don't you come? It'd be great to have you, and it's a fun afternoon."

"I'll let you know."

"You'd be able to meet some of the kids you've been helping."

"We'll see."

He frowned, knowing it was a no.

I logged on to my VPN and navigated to the website for the Florida Office of Insurance Regulation. Florida was one of a handful of states providing information on malpractice claims against a physician's malpractice policy.

Searching for Dr. Flagstaff yielded nothing. No patient had successfully sued the surgeon in the past decade.

The Florida Department of Health kept a record of complaints against doctors. Flagstaff had accumulated five in twenty years. None resulted in disciplinary action being taken against him.

This was a tough call. Barrone had suffered what appeared to be a permanent disability from the surgery. Whether it was an act of negligence was far from clear.

Flagstaff had an excellent reputation and a clean record. But he was human. We all make mistakes.

30

Despite making several inquiries, there was nothing substantive in Flagstaff's background indicating negligence or indifference. He was respected professionally. I made a call and headed to Vanderbilt Beach.

Laden with sand, a line of dump trucks crowded the cul-de-sac. They were waiting to add their load to the four-story mound being distributed by earthmoving equipment.

The sand was being moved north, toward Wiggins Pass. Larson, on the Ritz Carlton borderline, was seated far from the chaos.

He put down the *Wall Street Journal* and patted the empty chaise next to his. "Relax, Beck."

I pointed toward the replenishment. "That's some operation."

"It is. Costing the county twenty million. Let's hope it's worth it."

"It'll only last a couple of years, but tourism is the engine driving Florida."

"Not as much as it used to. The economy is really diversifying. Aviation and aerospace are growing, as are the information technology and medical fields."

"It's getting crowded down here."

"It is, but it's still the best place in the country. You want something to drink?"

"Nah. Look, I know Anna Barrone is a friend, and I'd love to help her, and you, but I don't think there's anything there."

He adjusted the back of his chair to a sitting position. "She's permanently disabled. You saw the way she walks."

"No doubt. Barrone has a bad case of drop foot, but I don't think we can blame the doctor."

"It was a direct result of the surgery. She doesn't get a hip replacement, she can run a marathon."

"If she was twenty years younger, I'd think you were dating her."

He frowned. "Flagstaff botched the operation, plain and simple."

"You're a lawyer; you know there was no evidence of negligence. You might be too close to this one."

"Flagstaff's partner's wife is related to the judge's sister."

"Okay, but where's the evidence Barrone didn't get a fair trial?"

Larson took a sip of his mineral water.

I said, "I feel sorry for Barrone, really, I do, but every procedure carries risks. She knew that; she signed the medical release forms."

"Not a soul on earth knows what they're signing as they're being wheeled into the operating room. That stuff wouldn't hold up in court."

"It won't if the surgeon was negligent. Flagstaff shows no signs of it. I don't see how I could help here."

"There's got to be something you can do to give her a little peace. She's going to limp around for the rest of her life."

Larson was as levelheaded as they came. This was out of character for him. He was also the most important contact I had. Meeting and working for him had been a godsend. Was there something I was missing? "I'll take another look at this."

"Good. You remember Ventura?"

"Phil, the lawyer?"

"Yes. You were working with me when he did some work for us."

"Yeah, sure. He's a good guy. What's up with him?"

"He's got something he needs help on."

"I don't know. I'm pretty booked."

"His client is a high-profile individual. It'll be worth your time."

DeRomo's was hopping. I weaved my way through the restaurant. Ventura was seated at an outdoor table overlooking a fountain. He smiled and stood. "Beck, how are you?"

"Good to see you."

He smiled. "It's good to be seen."

"Amen."

The waiter came over before my butt hit the seat. "Something to drink, gentlemen?"

Ventura ordered a glass of Chianti, and I said, "A Tito's on the rocks, please."

"I ordered some calamari. You want something else?"

"I'm good. So, how have you been?"

"Busy."

"You're still on your own, right?"

"Yes, I have two other lawyers working for me and a couple of paralegals. Luckily, we have more work than we can handle."

"Good for you."

The waiter set down our drinks.

I stirred my vodka with the straw. "Larson told me you needed help."

"It's nothing big, but one of my clients is upset. He feels like he's being taken for a ride. I have to agree with him, but we've been unable to crack this one."

I sipped my drink. "Fill me in."

"You know who Frank Puglia is?"

"The guy with all the dealerships?"

"Yes, he has three of them in town and a dozen others. Suffice it to say, he's wealthy. Lives on Gordon Drive, what a property, right on the beach. It's one of the nicest ones along that stretch."

The waiter set down a tray of fried calamari.

"What about him?"

"He was having his house painted, and one of the painters built a scaffold and fell. No one saw it happen, and the guy is claiming he hurt himself and is suing for five million."

"Why doesn't Puglia just settle it?"

"I told him to, but he wants to fight it to stop this type of thing from happening again. Word gets out he paid this guy, and people will not only be falling at his house, but he also fears it could spread to his dealerships."

"He has a point. People tend to target deep pockets."

"He sure does. If it goes to court, it'll get in the papers, and there's no telling how many others will follow." Ventura speared a ring. "Have some."

I forked a piece with arms. "More lawsuits are good for your business."

He frowned. "Puglia has some insurance, but believe it or not, he let his umbrella coverage lapse."

"How bad is this guy hurt?"

"We think he's faking it."

"Why?"

"We had our doctors examine him, and we can't find much. He's claiming nerve damage, giving him pain, and said his vision is blurry. Everything he complains about, we're unable to verify."

"What do you want me do?"

"Take a look into him. Work your magic; maybe you'll get lucky."

"Luck is what happens when preparation meets opportunity."

Ventura smiled. "Seneca, right?"

"Yep. What's the comp on this?"

"Puglia authorized up to a quarter of a million to make it go away."

"Nice. What's the painter's name?"

Ventura dug in his pocket, sliding a card across the table. "Rigo Munoz, here's his contact info."

"I'll get eyes on him, see if we can catch him off guard."

"Yeah, remember Beeson, the guy who got hit by the bike? He said he couldn't use his arms."

Smiling, I said, "Yep, caught him bowling up in Punta Gorda."

"Let's hope you can do something like that with Munoz."

31

I PARKED NEXT TO THE ANGULAR COLUMN JUTTING OFF THE Ferrari building. Expensive cars were lined up in the lot. I scanned the area for Caden.

A pair of yellow Lamborghinis stood out. The first thought I had was of how far the Italian manufacturer had come. Expanding my knowledge on exotic sports cars, I had watched a documentary on Lamborghini, who got his start building tractors. I shifted into wondering if one of the lemon-colored ones was owned by Caden.

Five groups of men were scattered around the lot, undoubtedly talking about cars. Sprinkled in two huddles were the guys I'd hired.

I approached a group surrounding a car I didn't know.

Fist-bumping someone I was paying to be there, I stood in front of a pasty green auto. It was a McLaren. I said, "A real beauty. What model is this?"

"A 720S."

"Nice. Anybody see Brett Caden?"

"Yeah, he's inside."

Heading into the showroom, I calculated there were over

thirty cars in the lot. With each worth over two hundred fifty thousand dollars, there was around ten million bucks of metal about to ride in formation.

Encircled by velvet ropes, an older model, with racing stripes, sat in the center of the showroom. Another antique, with a large number nine on its doors, testified to the cultlike following Ferrari had built over seventy-five years.

I checked the hood of a lime-green car that looked like it came out of a Marvel comic book. The prancing-horse logo confirmed it was a Ferrari.

Caden was at the far end of the huge, glass-walled space.

Passing a dozen works of automotive art, I waved to him. He and two men were standing next to a Formula One race car. The tires on the roadster were taller than the body of the car.

"Hey, Brett."

He stuck his hand out. "Beck, this is Dino. He's the general manager here."

We shook hands. "Nice to meet you."

Caden said, "Beck just broke his cherry; he picked up a used Portofino."

"We're proud to welcome you to the family."

A man in a royal-blue sports jacket approached. Caden said, "Look who's here, all the way from Maranello. How are you, Freddo?"

The man had a heavy, intriguing Italian accent. "Excellent. You, my friend?"

"Couldn't be better."

I palmed my phone as Caden said to me, "If you ever get a chance to go to Ferrari's factory, Freddo is the man. I've been there, like, six or seven times."

Freddo said, "It would be our pleasure to welcome you, anytime you wish to come, please let me know."

"We always have a blast. Remember how bombed we got at that restaurant up on the hill?"

As the Italian shook his head, saying, "Too much grappa. It took two days to recover." I hit my phone's record button to document the uniqueness of his voice.

"You're out of practice. Not me. The next day we had a special tasting in Antinori's personal wine cellar. We had, like, seven bottles of the best juice they ever made."

"I am told it is a wonderful, magical place. I have never been there."

"Really? I've been there half a dozen times."

I asked Freddo, "Your accent is wonderful. Where were you born?"

"Parma, about seventy-five kilometers from Maranello. It's a beautiful town famous for our prosciutto."

"Do you commute? How long a drive is it?"

"About an hour, but I'm always traveling, so it's not often I make the drive."

The general manager said, "It looks like they're getting ready to depart."

Drivers were climbing into their cars. My gaze settled on a tall, older man who inched his way into the gull-wing opening of a white Lamborghini. He was a decade past ownership age.

I said, "All right, let's get moving."

We filed outside and got into our respective cars. Caden, in a red Ferrari, was several cars ahead of mine. The procession rolled south on Route 41. The windshield and rearview mirror were filled with some of the best cars on the globe.

The group snaked its way onto Crayton Road. Every couple of minutes, a driver would pull out of the line and catapult ahead. The slingshot propulsion gave you a taste of the power underneath the gleaming hoods of the caravan.

The lead car weaved its way along the water, and after

finishing the drive on Gordon Drive, it was time for dinner. Two rows of the parking lot behind Tommy Bahama's were blocked off with red cones.

One by one, the exotic vehicles backed into parking spaces. More heads were turning and mouths gaping than at a show of scantily clad fashion models.

We headed to Barbatella. The group had reserved the ground floor of the outdoor restaurant. Caden was ahead of me. Two guys in the group approached him. They embraced. Caden knew quite a few of the people involved in the rally.

Caden walked toward Thirteenth Avenue. I headed toward the back entrance to the Old Naples Pub and cut through the building to the rear entrance of Barbatella.

I grabbed a table and kept my eyes on Third Street. Caden appeared a minute later, and I stood, motioning for him to sit with me.

As Caden took out a chair, I said, "You've been here before?"

"A thousand times. They have a decent wine list by the glass."

He flagged down a server and ordered a bottle of Brunello.

Two of the plants I hired to rile up Caden came to the table. I stood, introducing Caden to Jimmy Reilly and Bob Stone. They shook hands.

Reilly said, "That's a nice Aventador. I had one a couple years back."

Caden said, "What are you driving now?"

Reilly smiled. "Depends on the day."

"Me too. I've got a couple of Ferraris and a pair of Lambos, including the new Countach."

"I've got three of each and just picked up a Lotus."

Caden puffed his chest out. "Yeah, I used to have more cars, but now I focus on the best of the best, like my LaFerrari Aperta."

"The best is debatable. Right, Bob? You think McLaren is the tops."

Bob Stone said, "Depends on what you're looking for. I like speed, and nobody beats my McLaren 720S."

Caden said, "Maybe on a straightaway, but my 788 GTS gets the edge in handling and overall is faster."

Stone scoffed, "That's your opinion."

"Everybody knows that. It's not an opinion, it's fact. I ran it against a 788 GTS at the Miami Speedway in Homestead and won by five car lengths."

Caden sneered, "An English car could never beat an Italian one. The driver didn't know what he was doing."

I chimed in, "Maybe we'll have to have a race to settle this."

Caden picked up his menu. "Anytime. Any fucking time."

Stone said, "Jimmy, when are you shipping your car to Los Angeles?"

"Tomorrow."

"Yeah, me too. Probably on the same truck."

I said, "What's going on in LA?"

"The Concorso Italiano car show. The best cars Italy ever made will be there."

I asked Caden, "Are you putting any of yours in?"

Stone said, "It's by invitation only."

Caden said, "I'm starving. What are you getting to eat?"

32

Waiting for the dealer to open, I rehearsed what to say. At nine, I made a call.

"Ferrari of Naples."

"Hi, last night I was in your showroom. Well, really, I was there for the rally."

"How can I help you, sir?"

"I'm looking for Freddo, the manager from Maranello."

"He's on his way back to Italy."

"I know. He said to call him when I got there. I lost his cell number."

"I'm sorry, but I can't give that information out."

"Oh no. My wife and I are leaving tonight. You can ask Dino, he knows me. I just bought a Spider, and Freddo wanted to give me a tour of the factory."

"I'm really not supposed to . . . but okay."

"Please, I've dreamed of going to see how they make Ferraris since I was a little boy."

"All right, here's his number: 39-0536-949713."

"Thank you so much. We're really looking forward to the tour."

It was the last piece of the puzzle.

The short clip I'd taken of Freddo talking was all AI needed to train itself to mirror his voice. It was uncanny how easy it was, and equally, if not more so, terrifying. The ability to create deep fakes was going to become a major societal issue.

Following the instructions Larson's guy had given me, I input Freddo's number into an app on the phone. Any calls using the app would make it appear that the call was coming from Freddo's number.

I tapped in Caden's number. He picked up on the first ring. "Ciao, Freddo. How's my man doing?"

I had eight lines of text ready to convert into the voice of Freddo. I waited two seconds and hit the first one. "Ciao, Brett. We are all fine here. And you?"

"Doing good. What's going on?"

It was a perfect lead to another piece of prepared text. "The Concorso Italiano car show. The 250 GTO our Silicon Valley dealer was going to show was in an accident. We'd love to show your Aperta."

"Really?"

I typed. "Certo, it's magnificent."

"I know, it's a beauty."

"I need to know if you want to show it."

"Yeah, man. But why so late? Why wasn't I asked earlier?"

"I am so sorry. It was my mistake, too much traveling. I feel so bad last night, and, well, I hope you can forgive me."

"Of course. No worries. It's an honor, but the show is in, like, a couple of days, right? And it's in California."

"Yes, three days only. But we take care of everything. Ferrari will fly the car to Concorso."

"I'm in. What about the arrangements?"

"Perfecto. We come tomorrow to collect the car. If you like, get your ticket and we pay all expenses; just give to me the receipts."

"You going to be there?"

"Certo. I no miss Concorso in twenty years. Look, I must go. It is afternoon in Italy, and I have many things to do. I fly to London, then to US for show. If you need me, email is best."

"Safe travels. I'll see you in a couple of days."

The big smile on my face wilted when my phone rang. It was Caden. I hesitated and answered, "Hey, Brett. What's going on?"

"Just got a call from Freddo."

"Freddo?"

"The Ferrari guy from Italy."

"Oh yeah. What did he say?"

"Guess whose car they want in the Concorso show?"

"Yours?"

"Damn right. He said it was some kind of corporate screwup. They realized I wasn't in, and they're going to fly my car out."

"Wow. You going to go?"

"Absolutely. Why don't you come?"

"Isn't it in a few days?"

"Yeah."

"I'm working on a project."

"Push it off. It's only a couple of days. We'll do some partying."

"I can't. The guys running this one want what they want."

"Tell them to fucking wait a couple of days. The world's not going to end."

"You don't screw around with these guys. They're, you know, not the kind of guys you'd want your sister to marry."

"Gangsters?"

"You could say that. They're trying to go legitimate, but this one, uh, you're better off not knowing."

"But it's a good payday?"

"Oh yeah, really good, but, you know, it's risky."

"All right. You sure you can't come?"

"I'd like to, but I want to be around for a while."

"Okay."

"Enjoy the show."

"Yeah, and tell that loudmouth Stone my Aperta is in the show, and it'll probably snag the top trophy."

33

COCONUT POINT WAS JAMMED WITH SHOPPERS AND TOURISTS with nothing better to do on a sunny day. I walked past a dozen kids surrounding the outdoor mall's unique Turtle Pond.

It was impossible to miss Barrone as she limped her way toward me. I felt bad making her walk so far, but I'd been blinded by my hunger for a slice of Tony Sacco's pizza. Now, with a case of the repeats, I wasn't sure the Margherita pie was worth it.

"I'm sorry to make you come out here."

"It's fine. My daughter's birthday is coming up, and I wanted to see what Michael Kors had."

"Any luck?"

She shook her head. "I don't like their new look at all."

"You'll find something."

"I suppose you invited me here to tell me what you're going to do for me."

"I'm still conducting research."

She raised her leg. "Here's all the proof you need."

"Please don't misunderstand me; I'm not doubting your condition."

"No one could."

"It must have been difficult for you. I mean, you must have been in a lot of pain to get a new hip."

"Oh, the pain was terrible. I couldn't walk, but I avoided getting a replacement. I used to ask the orthopedic doctors when I should get it done, and everyone said the same thing, 'You'll know when it's time.'"

"When you can't stand the pain any longer?"

"Exactly."

"It was that bad?"

"Unbearable at times. I ruined my stomach by taking Advil to deal with it and stopped going out. My son came to visit, and he started making calls, insisting I go to Dr. Flagstaff."

"He found the surgeon?"

"Yep." She pointed at her foot. "And now I got this."

"You get around fine."

"I should've gone to somebody else. All Flagstaff cared about was his daughter's wedding. That's all he talked about."

"She was getting married?"

"Yeah, the Saturday before my surgery on Monday."

"Every parent, if they like the person their kid is marrying, gets excited. I wouldn't read too much into it."

"That butcher disfigured me. He didn't give one damn about me."

It wasn't disfigurement, but it was senseless to argue. My strength wasn't in rationalizing, it was in equalizing things as best as I could.

My silence prompted her to ask, "Are you going to do something about it?"

"As I mentioned, I'm in discovery mode."

"What's there to discover? You know what he did to me."

I stood. "I've been doing what I do for some time now. One

thing I've learned is to take my time. I know people want things done quickly, but that's not how I operate."

"Okay, I understand, but don't let it drag on forever."

"Enjoy this beautiful day, Anna."

Walking through the mall, I saw a woman duck into the West Elm store. From the back, she looked like Laura. I hustled over and entered the store. She was opening drawers on a dresser.

Her hair was the same color and length of Laura's. Walking over, I cleared my throat. She turned around, and I made like I was interested in a club chair. It wasn't her.

I left the store. Heading to my car, I debated calling Laura. She was as stubborn as they came. Forgetting to call seemed like nothing to me, yet she was still pissed. Was there something I was missing? I pulled out my phone.

She wanted to send a message, which I got, but she was acting like I'd hacked off one of her arms.

Suddenly she was two different people. Easygoing Laura had vanished, replaced by a stonewalling stranger. I didn't need this bullshit. I tucked the phone away.

There was nothing wrong with being private. My life wasn't an open book; it was complicated and nobody's business. If she couldn't understand that, it wouldn't work out.

My burner buzzed. It was Mario. "Hey, what's up?"

"Where are you?"

"Estero. Why?"

"I've been watching this Munoz guy, but either he's careful, or the dude is really hurt."

"What's he up to?"

"For one, he's always wearing the neck brace thing. I can't see inside the house, but anytime he comes out front, he's wearing it."

"Are you watching the lanai?"

"Yeah, I put up a drone, but when he goes out there, he's got it on."

"Keep watching him."

"You sure? This guy moves around like he's hurting."

"People will do a lot for five million."

"I know, but I'm thinking it may be a legit claim. You should see him yourself."

"That'd be a shame. There's a quarter of a million riding on it."

"Like you say, accept things as they are."

"Almost, wise guy. The stoics say to concern yourself with the things under your control and let the universe handle things that aren't."

Mario said, "The trick is to figure out which is which."

"If you're honest with yourself, you'll know what things or situations you can affect."

"Whatever. If you have time, you need to see this guy."

"I'm going to check the doctors he went to. Let me see what develops."

Ventura and his wealthy client were convinced it was a scam. Puglia had the dough to make the case disappear but wouldn't settle. Was he worried about people lining up to sue him? Or did he believe it was just plain wrong?

There were always two, if not three, sides to every story. In half the cases I handled, the people who wanted things squared either bore responsibility or were mistaken about the circumstances they asked help for.

It wasn't easy telling people who felt wronged that I couldn't make it right. At times, the person they wanted revenge on wasn't at fault, or it was debatable what role they played.

My phone rang. It was Larson. I asked him, "Hey, how'd it go?"

"Good. Caden took me to the Lamborghini dealer. He's a piece of work."

"Tell me about it."

"And man, can he drink. I left him at Blue Martini at one last night."

"You're best buds now."

Larson scoffed, "You are going to owe me. Look, I'm outside Whole Foods. I just wanted to update you. We'll talk later."

Another building block was in place. Now it was time to put my plan in place to give to Puzo what he had dished out to others. Fingering the scar behind my ear, I waited for the call I had placed to be answered.

34

Singing along with the new Keith Urban song, I hopped over the back of the couch and plopped onto it. The TV was muted. As the five-o'clock news introduction began, I tapped the Sonos app, switching the sound from music to the TV.

The anchor said, "In an ironic turn of events, a prominent lawyer found himself on the other side of the law. Our Melissa Wright is in Port Royal. Melissa, this is a surprising development in the legal community."

"Shocking is more like it, Bob. I'm standing in front of the Galleon Drive home owned by William Puzo. Acting on a tip, the Collier County Sheriff's Office raided the recently renovated home. Mr. Puzo, a prominent defense attorney, was arrested earlier today and is awaiting arraignment on drug possession with intent to distribute."

I rubbed the scar behind my ear as the reporter continued. "Mr. Puzo, who has successfully represented several people accused of being drug dealers, now finds himself on the other side of the table facing the same serious charges his clients do.

"*WINK News* spoke with Sheriff Rambosk, who said his office was committed to keeping the county as drug free as possible. The sheriff praised his officers for the investigation and arrest.

"Mr. Puzo is scheduled to be arraigned later today."

The news anchor interjected, "This is a fascinating case. Is there any information on whether Mr. Puzo will represent himself?"

"We'll find out later, but if Mr. Puzo is convicted, he'll not only be disbarred, he'll also be facing significant jail time."

"Thank you, Melissa. *WINK* is going to follow this case, informing you of the developments. And now we're going to get a report from our Los Angeles affiliate station on the current state of the wildfires raging just outside the city."

I shut off the TV and put the music back on. The dopamine high from nailing Puzo started wearing away. It never lasted long enough.

Grabbing my phone off the cocktail table, I made a call.

"Collier County Prosecutor's Office. How may I direct your call?"

"Prosecutor O'Leary."

After two rings, O'Leary picked up. "John O'Leary."

"Hey. Can you call me back?"

"Give me five."

Pacing the lanai, I thought about Puzo. The sleazebag was in hot water, but there was no way he was going to prison. O'Leary had said they'd negotiate a plea.

My burner vibrated. "Hey."

"What's up?"

"Puzo. Just want to make sure everything is on track."

"It's early, he's not even arraigned yet."

"I know, but I want to make sure nobody is making a bigger deal out of it than it already is."

"So far it's an avalanche of gossip."

"It's got to stay that way."

O'Leary exhaled. "Puzo stepped on a lot of toes."

"I need you to keep it on track."

"We should be okay."

"I don't want to hear the word *should.* Puzo has no history of dealing or a record. His furniture was in storage, his house was under renovation and—"

"As long as he says it was for personal use and agrees to give up his law license, he'll probably get a suspended sentence."

"Who's representing him?"

"He's repping himself."

"That's usually not a good idea. But in this case, it might help."

35

After rehearsing what he was going to say, Larson dialed a number. Caden answered on the first ring. "Yo, Larson, how's it going? That was some time we had, huh?"

"I had a bad headache the next day."

"You got to practice."

Larson laughed. "How are you doing?"

"Perfect. Never been better."

"Good."

"What's up? You ready to jump into Lambo land?"

"I'm thinking of it. That Aventador is something else."

"Pull the trigger, man. You won't regret it."

"The price is up there. I'm leaning toward the Huracan."

"If you do that, it's got to be the Huracan HTO. Forget the EVO model."

"I know. I remember what you said about it."

"I can take you back to the dealer. They know me, might be able to swing a deal for you."

"Thanks. Where are you?"

"Angelwax, getting my Spider pampered. You get a Lambo,

you got to get an Angelwax coating. It protects the finish and shines like the sun."

"So, you can't talk?"

"No, I can. What's up?"

"You know I have a lot of contacts in law enforcement."

"Sure. You said you used to be a cop and a lawyer."

"You remembered? I thought after all the partying the other night you would have forgotten."

"It takes more than three bottles of wine and a couple of tequila shots to put me down." He laughed. "What's the deal with the law enforcement stuff?"

"Well, I just ran into a prosecutor I worked with for several years. I was telling him about the possibility of getting a Lamborghini, and your name came up. I said you knew Italian cars inside out."

"Your buddy wants to get one?"

"No, but, uh, he told me something in confidence that I, uh, felt you should know."

"Spit it out. What did he say?"

"Well, I swore I wouldn't say anything, so, you have to promise not to let it get back to him or anybody, okay?"

"I can keep a fucking secret. Get to it."

"Puzo, he was your lawyer, when you had that accident, right?"

Caden hesitated. "Yeah, what about him?"

Larson lowered his voice. "He's in deep water. They found a significant amount of drugs at his house."

"What's that got to do with me?"

"I hear he's talking to position himself, you know, trying to make a deal to get off or lower the charges."

"Typical of lawyers. They'll sell out to anybody, the self-interested pieces of shit. I feel bad for the poor bastards he's selling out."

"That's the thing, I was told he mentioned your name."

"M-m-me?"

"That's what he said."

Caden paused. "In connection with what?"

"The accident."

He recovered quicker than an Olympic figure skater. "Puzo can say what he wants. There's nothing to talk about."

"Really? The prosecutor said Puzo claimed he set you up with a doctor who faked the stress fracture and that—"

"Fuck this bullshit! Puzo wants to shoot off his mouth about shit, let him. Look, I gotta go, my car's ready."

"Hang on a second."

"What?"

"I wouldn't be calling Puzo when he gets out of jail. He'd be considered a witness, and they'll charge you with obstruction."

"Why would I call that piece of shit?"

"Just making sure you don't get caught up in anything."

It was no surprise that Flagstaff's best friend was another doctor. Whether it was the god complex, or that nobody else could understand what they did was immaterial, surgeons liked to pal around with each other.

A couple of years younger than Flagstaff, Dr. Valencia was bald. Was it the stress of neurosurgery, or bad genetics? He smoothed the front of his white coat. "I'm surprised NCH didn't send anything out."

I flipped open my legal pad. "It's not coming out until next year. There are quite a few doctors to interview. It's more of a behind-the-scenes look, you know, to humanize the physicians on staff."

"It sounds like a valuable effort."

"We think it will help foster better confidence in patients."

He smiled. "Maybe they'll go back to getting just two opinions."

"It's the internet. Everybody is an expert."

"No doubt. It's good that patients are informed and research their conditions, but many have gone overboard."

"I'm sure you see that. So, let's get started."

"Fire away."

"Do you mind if I record this?"

"Not at all."

"Good. Tell me when you decided you wanted to dedicate your life to helping others?"

"I remember it vividly. I had just celebrated my ninth birthday and my grandmother was diagnosed with leukemia. We didn't have the tools we have today, and it was heartbreaking. The care she received wasn't terrible, but I felt it could have been better and decided to become a physician."

"I like the family angle to this. Now, tell me about the med school you attended and your internship and residency experiences."

After ten minutes, I cut the doctor off. "Let's change things up and go personal. Tell me about your family life."

The surgeon had a wife of thirty-nine years, three adult daughters, and four grandkids.

"I understand you're very friendly with Dr. Flagstaff?"

"Oh yes. We've went to med school together and formed a bond right away."

"I'm going to interview him as well. Can you give me any personal insights that would help?"

"He's a great guy, loves to golf, but like all of us, he doesn't get out as often as he'd like."

"I understand his daughter was married recently."

"Yes, it was fantastic. Flagstaff went for his lungs. The affair was at the Ritz by the beach."

"Wow. You had a good time?"

"We did. But I was hurting the next day."

"Too much drinking?"

"Definitely. Flagstaff is into wine, and we must have had three bottles of Californian cult wines between us."

"No wonder you were hungover. Do you and Dr. Flagstaff share wine often?"

"Not for years. We both lost the ability to snap back. These days, it's only special occasions, like the wedding."

"Father Time wins again."

"He sure does."

I lowered my voice. "I've interviewed many surgeons, and the job is so demanding, they need, should we say, an outlet. Some lean toward drugs—"

"Not me."

"What about Dr. Flagstaff?"

"Absolutely not, or at least not in the thirty-plus years I've known him."

"It's not for the article, but I'm curious, what about marital infidelity?"

"I've been faithful to my wife."

"Good. I heard Dr. Flagstaff had a fling or two."

"I think you're mistaken."

Was something there? I had to get back to Valencia's professional career or he'd get suspicious.

36

A TRUCK, EMBLAZONED WITH THE LOGO OF THE HORSELESS Carriage, was parked in front of Caden's home. While the driver went to Caden's front door, two others got out of the cab and opened the trailer's rear doors.

Caden greeted the driver. "Morning. I'll meet you by the garage."

The men began assembling a long ramp as the garage door rolled up. "You want me to drive it out?"

"That's okay, sir. We got it from here."

"Be careful, her ground clearance is under five inches."

He pointed toward the rear of the truck. "Yes, sir. Our ramp has a very gradual incline."

"Are you taking her straight to the airport?"

"Yes, sir. We're leaving straight for Miami." He put his hand on the door handle. "May I?"

Caden handed him a red key fob. "Sure."

He watched the man slowly drive his prize possession behind the truck. One of the men walked up the ramp into the trailer and the other helped the driver line up with the ramp.

"Okay, come on up."

The Ferrari inched its way onto the trailer. With Caden looking on, they secured the truck and closed the doors. The driver handed Caden a clipboard. "We'll need you sign this, sir."

Caden scribbled his signature without reading anything. "Be careful with my baby."

"No worries, sir."

Caden brightened as he passed the sign for Monterey and took the exit for Seaside, California. The road was curvy and he slowed down. The convertible Porsche 911 handled decently, but it was no Ferrari.

As he took the access road for Bayonet Golf Course, Caden mused about winning the award for best of the show. His Aperta was highly sought after, but most past winners were older, vintage cars.

As he parked, he settled on getting the Chairman's Award. It'd be impossible to bypass his car. Caden dug into his jeans and pulled out a vial. He looked around, bent over, and snorted two hits. He checked the rearview mirror, pocketed the coke, and got out.

Pumped, Caden strode onto the sea of emerald-green grass toward rows and rows of gleaming vehicles. This was going to be a hell of a great day.

Looking for a familiar face, he strolled up to the registration tent.

"Welcome to Concorso Italiano. What is your name, sir?"

"Sir? I'm Brett. Brett Caden."

"Just a moment." She scanned three pages of names. "Hmm. How do you spell that?"

"C-A-D-E-N. My first name is Brett."

She looked again. "I'm sorry, sir. I don't see your name. Did you preregister?"

"Look again. My Ferrari Aperta is in the show."

She ran her finger down the names on each sheet of paper. "It's not here. Maybe there's been some kind of mistake."

"Freddo Romano invited me. He's the North American brand manager. Check under his name, I'm probably there."

The woman scanned the list. "Romano with an R?"

"Of course!"

"I'm sorry, he isn't listed either. Are you at the right show?"

"What the hell kind of question is that? What do you think, I'm some of kind of idiot?"

"No, sir. Don't get upset, I'm trying to help."

"This is bullshit! Who's your boss? Get me somebody who can help."

Two men in gray jackets approached the table. "Sir, we're going to have to ask you to calm down."

"Look, my car, a frigging Ferrari Aperta, is in the show, and you can't find me in your shitty system?"

"Why don't we step aside and let the others check in? We'll figure this out together, okay?"

Caden exhaled and followed the men to a tent marked Security.

One of them slipped behind a table and asked, "What's your name, sir?"

"I told that girl. Brett Caden."

The man plugged his name into a laptop. "We don't have a record—"

"This is bullshit. Ferrari asked to use my car for the show. Who is here from Ferrari?"

"There are many representatives from Ferrari."

Caden pulled out his phone. "Forget it. The brand manager

and me are good friends." He pulled up the number of Freddo Romano and called it.

"Freddo, where are you? I'm getting dicked around by a Walmart cop."

"Brett?"

"Yeah, I'm standing near registration. Where are you?"

"I'm home, in Maranello."

"You're not coming to Concorso Italiano?"

"No."

"You told me you were gonna be here."

"When? We haven't talked since I was in Naples."

"You called me three days ago."

"I'm sorry, but I didn't."

"What the fuck are you talking about? You asked for my Aperta, for the show."

"I'm sorry, but I don't know what you refer to."

The security officers drew nearer to Caden as he said, "Are you fucking with me?"

"It's late in Italy. I was just going to sleep."

"Where's my fucking car?"

"I don't know what you are talking about?"

"You don't fucking know? You sent a truck, Horseless Carriage, to my house to pick it up."

"We don't use them in the United States. We prefer—"

"Stop with the fucking games. Where is my car?"

"Brett, are you feeling okay?"

The security guards encircled Caden. One said, "Sir, we're going to have to ask you to leave."

"Fuck you. Fuck everybody!"

They grabbed him by the elbow. "We'll escort you out."

Caden shook them off and headed toward the rows of cars. "I don't need no fucking escort. I'm going to find my car."

One of guards called for the police, who had stationed a car near the golf course's clubhouse.

Caden was steps away from a double row of classic red Ferraris. A golf cart swerved into his path. A police officer hopped out. "Sir, you're going to have to come with me."

"You don't understand; my car is here. All I'm trying to do is find it."

"You're not registered at this event, and that means you're trespassing. If you refuse to leave, I'll have to arrest you."

"Hey, man. My Ferrari is here. I got a right to be here."

"Sir, I'm going to ask you one more time to leave."

"I'm not going anywhere. My Ferrari is worth more than you'll earn in your whole, pathetic lifetime."

"Put your hands behind your back, sir."

37

YESTERDAY I'D SCOURED THE INTERNET BUT COULDN'T FIND any news. Was it too early? Or considering the amount of crime in California, too insignificant to cover? It was time to go local. I navigated to the *Monterey Herald.*

The front page featured an overhead picture, taken by a drone, of scores of shiny cars dotting the fairways of a golf course. I clicked to the next page and there it was: "Florida Man Arrested at Concorso Italiano Car Show."

My hand went behind my ear as I read the small piece:

Responding to a disturbance, police arrested a man trespassing at the Italian exotic car show. Brett Caden, the Florida man brought into custody, was also charged with possession of an illegal narcotic.

The corners of my mouth rose; this was better than expected. I continued reading.

According to witnesses, Mr. Caden was acting erratically. It is unknown whether he was under the influence of a substance at the time of his arrest. Mr. Caden is being held at the Monterey County Jail and awaits a psychiatric evaluation.

It was easy to picture Caden going off the deep end when he

realized he'd been scammed out of one of the world's most valuable cars. What wasn't predictable was the drug charge. This wasn't foreseen and could screw things up.

I used a burner to call Larson. "Can you talk?"

"Sure. What's going on?"

I filled him in on Caden's arrest and asked, "What's going to happen with the drug charges?"

"I'm not an expert on California's code, but it's going to depend on the amount of drugs he was carrying."

"I can't believe he got on a plane carrying coke."

"You're sure it was cocaine?"

"Ninety-nine percent. He's always snorting that crap."

"With all cocaine being laced with fentanyl, he's playing Russian roulette."

"Everybody is. If it's coke, what kind of trouble is he in?"

"Assuming it's for personal consumption, and he's a first-time offender, he'll probably plead it down and end up paying a fine."

"And the trespassing?"

"Misdemeanor. This is California; he may not even get a fine."

"That works. How long do you think he'll be tied up in California?"

"With the right counsel, he'll be out on bail after whatever court-mandated evaluation is completed."

"Would that be quick?"

"It's just an interview by a psychiatrist. Shouldn't take long if they don't find anything."

Was narcissism a jailable offense? "Then he can leave the state?"

"They can work that out. He'll be released. We're not talking about a murderer."

I thought we were. "Did you get rid of it?"

"It's on the way to Russia."

"And the money?"

"It was sent anonymously to Mothers Against Drunk Driving this morning."

"Thanks."

"Anytime. When am I getting my car back?"

"Don't worry, I just need a little more time."

After hanging up, I composed a short text to Caden: *Hey, hope the show was good. When you get over the jet lag, give me a shout. I'd like to take you up on your offer to go with me to the Ferrari dealer.*

It was more than likely that Caden's phone had been confiscated upon booking. I'd wait a day before sending another text. Speaking to Caden would provide clues on how he was handling his predicament.

The waiting room at Dr. Yushenko's office was half full. I went to the receptionist. "Hey, Denise. How are you?"

"Good. He's really busy."

"Tell him I need five minutes, that's it. Maybe less."

She frowned and picked up the phone. Ten minutes later, she waved me through a side door.

Yushenko was carrying a file. "I'm extremely busy."

"I know. We can do this here." I lowered my voice. "If someone is drunk, very drunk, how long would they be impaired?"

"There is no simple answer. Besides how much they drank, other factors such as what their tolerance is, were they eating, how much they weigh—"

"Okay. Generally speaking, someone with a medium build in his fifties drinks a bottle and a half of wine, maybe more."

"Do they consume alcohol regularly?"

"No. Only on special occasions."

"Well, my guess is they'd be rather hungover the next day, if not sick."

"What about the day after that? Say the overdrinking occurred on a Saturday. What would Monday morning look like? Would you still be drunk or hungover?"

"You wouldn't be drunk; the half-life of alcohol is four to five hours. So, it takes your body about twenty-five hours to metabolize alcohol."

"But is it possible to be hungover?"

"Sure. You'd have slept poorly, so you'd be tired and dehydrated. Possibly less focused, and your coordination might suffer as a result of these factors."

I squeezed a pair of Benjamins in his hand. "Thanks, Doc."

Larson answered the door. "Come on in, Beck."

"No beach today?"

"Too windy."

"You can't nap when the wind is blowing?"

"Very funny. Wait ten years, you'll see there's nothing like a good nap."

I followed him into the kitchen. His island had quartz waterfalls. "Look, I wanted to talk to you about Barrone."

He sat down. "You got something?"

"Not really. Bottom line is there's a possibility the surgeon might have been a little off the morning of the surgery."

"That's all it takes."

I shrugged. "It's paper-thin. Flagstaff was drunk at his daughter's wedding, but it was Saturday and started at five.

Yushenko said he could have been dehydrated, but most doctors hook up an IV bag when they get bombed."

"They do?"

"I've heard that before. If he stopped drinking by nine, it'd be almost thirty-six hours before he was in the operating room."

"There's nothing else on him?"

"No. I looked under every rock. It's borderline at best. I know this is a special case for you. Maybe we can do something small, like setting off Flagstaff's smoke alarms or—"

"You don't think it was Flagstaff's fault?"

"I really don't."

"Okay. Drop it."

"You sure?"

"Yes."

"You want me to tell her?"

"I'll tell her myself. You have enough on your hands."

38

Caden opened the door. "Hurry, come in."

I slipped inside and he closed the door.

"Man, I can't believe it. You got arrested?"

"Motherfuckers said I was trespassing. They couldn't cut me some slack? I got ripped off."

He could store a week's worth of clothes in the bags under his eyes. "We got to be able to do something. Tell me what happened."

Caden pawed the stubble on his face. "It's like a movie, you know, or a dream or something."

I followed him into the family room. The drapes were drawn. "What happened?"

Sitting on the coffee table was a mirror and the remnants of cocaine. He paced the room. "Freddo called, he wanted the Aperta in the Concorso show."

"Yeah, I remember you told me."

"It had to be somebody imitating his voice. It's so fucked up, man." He wet his finger and swiped granules of coke off the mirror, rubbing it along his upper gums. "I got out to the show, and Freddo wasn't there, and neither was my fucking Aperta. I got scammed. It's so fucked up!"

"I don't understand. How could they take your car? It's worth a ton, no?"

"Five million."

"Holy shit! You have insurance, right?"

He scoffed. "It was insured for two million. The motherfuckers are giving me a hard time."

"Why only two million?"

"I don't know. I paid like just over three and a half, and the agent, she was telling me I could save money. I didn't care, but I went along with what she said."

"They got to be able to find the car. It's so rare, it'll stand out."

Caden mumbled, "The cops said it was probably out of the country already."

"Or maybe it was a car kidnapping thing. Somebody might be asking for a ransom."

"You think so?"

"Sure, it could be."

"Nah, they would've reached out already. And the cops are sure it's been shipped overseas."

"Maybe, but Ferrari has some kind of registry. It has to show up sooner or later."

He went into the kitchen. "It's fucking gone. And I got to deal with the fucking drug charge in California."

"You said you were getting it reduced to a misdemeanor."

"I am, but this shit is going to follow me. I can feel it."

"What do you mean?"

"I was set up, man."

"By who?"

He reached into a cannister and came out with a glassine envelope of coke. "How the fuck do I know?"

"I know you're upset, but maybe you should lay off that stuff for a while."

"Don't tell me what to do. Okay?"

I checked the time. Mario was going to call him any minute. "I'm just looking out for you, bro."

"I can take care of myself."

The evidence was contrary to his belief. "I know. I just don't want to see you so down."

"I'm not down. I'm just trying to figure out what the hell happened."

Caden's cell phone rang. "It's a restricted number, these frigging robocalls."

"Answer it. It might be the people who took your car."

"You think so?"

"Definitely. Put it on speaker."

Caden set the phone on the kitchen table and hit the speaker. "Yeah?"

The color drained from his face as Mario read from the script we'd created. "Mr. Caden, I'm with the Collier County Attorney's Office."

"What's this about? My car?"

"No, sir. You were involved in a fatal car accident."

He flopped onto a chair. "That was a long time ago."

"A witness has come forward challenging large segments of the evidence you presented during trial."

"I, I don't know what you're talking about."

"What we're talking about is falsifying medical records and other documentation to avoid a conviction for vehicular manslaughter."

"I really don't know anything. My lawyer was in charge. He handled everything. You have to talk to William Puzo."

"We already have."

"What did he tell you?"

"We're unable to reveal the discussions we have with witnesses."

"What do you want with me?"

"At this point, Mr. Caden, we're simply advising you that we've opened an investigation into the matter."

"W-w-what does that mean?"

"We're going to examine the entire case and determine whether it was properly adjudicated. Enjoy the rest of your day, Mr. Caden."

The phone clicked, and Caden put his head in his hands. "I'm fucked. What am I going to do?"

"So, Puzo did open his mouth."

"He's selling me out to save his ass."

"Maybe you should call him?"

"I called the bastard ten times. He's avoiding me."

"That's not a good sign. You know, I'm just wondering—nah, it can't be."

He stood. "What? What can't be?"

I said, "It's crazy, but do you think there's a chance Puzo was involved in the car scam?"

"I don't know . . . I guess."

He opened the freezer and took out a bottle of GREY GOOSE Vodka. "You want a drink?"

"Just a taste."

He poured four fingers in a glass, took a large gulp and spilled out a splash for me. "Puzo is a scumbag. I never liked the bastard."

"I heard he's a great lawyer, and he did get you off."

"So? That doesn't mean I liked him."

"Puzo is really connected. He knows a lot of people."

He threw back the rest of his drink. "Why would he be picking on me?"

"He's in hot water and looking to trade information to get a better deal."

"I can't fucking believe he's dredging up the accident."

"Let me ask you, does he have anything that could make you look bad?"

"There was a lot of shit going on back then."

"I don't understand; what does that mean?"

"Nothing. Forget about it. Maybe I should get a lawyer."

"No. I wouldn't do that."

"Why not?"

"It'll be a signal you're hiding something."

Caden shrugged. "It don't matter. They're looking into this already."

"You know, I'm just thinking, you know about double jeopardy?"

"Kinda. I remember a movie I saw a while back."

"Well, if someone is on trial and they get acquitted, they can't be charged again."

Caden's eyes widened. "Holy shit. That's right."

"You have nothing to worry about."

"But what if they find new evidence?"

"I don't think it matters. Let me Google it." I tapped on my phone. "You're home free, my friend. The only time double jeopardy doesn't apply is if the judge or jury was bribed. You don't know about any bribes, do you?"

He smiled. "No, nothing like that." He grabbed the bottle and drank from it. "Beck, you're a fucking genius."

39

Dr. Yushenko shook his head as he entered the exam room. "You are killing your liver."

I smiled. "Not here for that, Doc. I have a couple of questions about something."

"Well, that's welcome news. What can I do for you?"

"You're a neurological specialist, right?"

"Yes, believe it or not, my specialty isn't hydrating patients."

"Touché. Can you give me a crash course on nerve damage."

"That doesn't exist. We're just beginning to understand—"

"I got it, Doc. Let's say someone falls off a ladder and claims they suffered nerve damage. Is that realistic?"

"Naturally, the height you fall from would impact the severity of an injury, but you can get hurt stepping off a curb."

"He was on a six-foot ladder. Let's say he was five feet off the ground. Would that cause nerve damage?"

"This is very speculative, but blunt force trauma can damage your nerves by compressing them."

"What about damaging the neck area?"

"Whiplash is not normally associated with falls, but a harsh jerking of the head could result in it."

"What kind of pain is possible?"

"Nerve damage is known to cause some of the worst pain a human can experience. It can be quite debilitating."

"What kind of proof is there of nerve damage? Is there a test of some kind?"

"There are a couple of tests, but they're not definitive. Some cases are exceedingly difficult to diagnose."

"Is it common for doctors to disagree on a diagnosis?"

"As I mentioned at the outset, we're still learning and have a long way to go. Consensus may differ, but we start with the patient and their symptoms."

"Which ones are difficult to nail down a cause?"

"Whiplash has always been challenging, but we always err on the side of caution, immobilizing the neck to prevent additional damage."

"What else?"

"Uncontrolled muscle movements are difficult to pinpoint."

"Is it possible to fake nerve damage?"

He frowned. "Would you like me to examine someone?"

"That's not going to happen. But can you tell me if it is possible to fake the pain and pass it off as nerve damage?"

"People have varying degrees of pain tolerance. What you might be able to push through, others may be unable to tolerate."

"Why is that? We're biologically the same."

"The simple answer is we don't know. We're learning every day, but we don't know much about the brain and the neurological system."

A steady breeze cooled Food for Thought's outdoor deck. Focusing on their turkey club sandwich, I followed the hostess. She stopped at a table and dropped a menu. "Have a good lunch."

"This is my table?"

"It's all yours."

I hesitated. "Thanks."

It was the same table Laura and I had eaten at each of the four times we'd come here. Dismissing the thought that it was some kind of message, the server came to take my order. It was the tattooed girl we'd had every time.

"Hey, there. Are we waiting on your friend?"

"Uh, no. Flying solo. I'd like the turkey club and a seltzer."

"You got it."

I pulled my phone out and scrolled to the text string with Laura. The last one was days ago. It was nearing the point of no return. I ping-ponged ideas and typed, *Hey, how's it going?* Reading it back, I deleted it.

The server brought my lunch. "You must really like this sandwich; you always get it."

"If you find something you like, why change it?"

She laughed and walked away.

It tasted great. It always did. Even Laura, who religiously ordered a salad when out and wasn't a fan of turkey, had one for lunch the last time we were here. I tried to remember the joke she said that afternoon.

I'd choked on my food when she delivered the punch line. It had something to do with a zebra who thought he was a lion. When she told a joke, she'd giggle, making every word seem funny.

I gobbled the rest of my lunch and paid. As soon as I got in the car, I pulled my phone out and composed a text to Laura:

We need to talk. Call me when you can. I erased it and pushed the button to start the car.

What I'd typed could be interpreted in several ways. It was perfect. I retyped it and hit send. I dialed up the air-conditioning and played with the radio. Three songs later, the phone hadn't rung. She was probably busy.

I pocketed the phone and headed to see Caden.

---

iPad in hand, Caden answered the door. "Beck, what's going on?"

"I was in the neighborhood, and I figured I'd get your opinion on something."

"Sure. What do you need?"

"It's going to sound crazy, but I'm thinking of getting another Ferrari."

He smiled. "Far from it, man. You caught the bug, that's all. You'd be surprised how many guys get their second ride within a year of breaking their cherry."

"Really?"

"Yeah, come in. Tell me what you're thinking."

"I really like this place. Is this real wood?"

"Of course."

"I never saw it so white."

"It's nice, isn't it?"

"Yeah, but how do you keep it clean?"

"I don't worry about it. It gets looking shabby, I'll have it ripped out and have something else put in."

I followed him onto the rear deck. "That's the way to do it."

"How do you like this view? Pretty sweet, isn't it?"

"You have a boat?"

"I've got my eye on a few."

"Good luck."

"What Ferrari are you looking at?"

"The Roma."

He shook his head. "Nah, you don't want one of those. They pulled the plug on the Portofino to make the Roma Spider."

"They did?"

"Yeah, the Roma is an entry-level rari. You need to upgrade."

My phone vibrated. "To what?"

"Oh, you got plenty of choices."

"I don't want to break the bank."

"What are you worried about? You can't take it with you. I gotta take a leak."

"Okay." I snuck a peek—Laura was calling. I answered, "Hey, can I call you right back?"

She was crying. The last thing I needed was emotional incontinence.

I asked her what was wrong, and when she told me, my body stiffened. "I'm on the way."

40

THE LIGHTS OF A POLICE CAR BOUNCED OFF THE BUILDINGS making up Vanderbilt Collections. I pulled into a spot as the cop drove away.

Mario was sitting on a bench. Laura was standing over him. I hustled over. "Are you feeling okay?"

"Yeah, a headache is coming on, but I'm all right."

"You should go to the hospital."

"No. I don't need to."

"What happened?"

Mario shifted the hand holding a bag of ice on the top of his head. "I was going to get a slice at Mister O1, and next thing I know—bam—I get hit on the head."

Shorts hugging her curves, Laura said, "I saw the whole thing. I was going to get my bikini wax" (My groin ached. I didn't need the distraction) "and didn't even know it was Mario. I saw this guy coming around from the back of the building. He had his hand on the wall. I realized it was Mario, and then a motorcycle came flying between the buildings and took off."

"Did you get a look at the driver?"

She said, "Not really. He had, like, a bandanna over the bottom of his face."

Mario said, "I was stunned, but from the back he reminded me of that guy, Hound."

"Royal's guy?"

He nodded.

"You sure?"

"I think so."

"He say anything?"

"No, nothing."

I turned to Laura. "Anything you can tell me about who it might have been?"

"Who is Hound?"

"Some guy we know."

"See? You can't even tell me about some random guy who might have hit Mario."

"No. That's not it. I'm just trying to figure out what the hell happened and why."

"Who is Hound?"

"If it's him, he used to work with Royal."

"The man who died when his boat blew up?"

I nodded.

"Why would they attack Mario?"

I shrugged. "I have no idea."

She scoffed, "Nothing changes with you, Beck."

"No, don't misunderstand me."

"I have to go. I'm late already."

I watched her perfect ass walk away. Any chance that I'd see the wax technician's work evaporated.

Mario said, "I can see you didn't patch it up with her."

"Not yet. You sure you're okay?"

"I'm fine. A headache, but that's it."

"You can't take chances. I'll call Dr. Yushenko. We have to make sure you don't have a concussion."

"Who is going to keep on eye on the painter?"

"You said you thought he was really hurt."

"That's what I think."

"I'll swing by later and check him out myself."

"You want the drone? It's in my car."

"Nah, I'll wing it."

We climbed into my car. I backed out of the space, saying, "If this is Royal's guy, it might be payback for killing his alibi."

"Why would they give a shit about that now?"

"Loyalty. Could be a struggle for control, and these guys are vying to show who'd carry on in Royal's place."

"Maybe it was just some nutjob."

"I don't like the fact he used a motorcycle to get away. Royal's crew uses them in a lot of their hanky-panky."

Driving along Airport Pulling Road, I reviewed the sequence of events. Things turned quickly. Laura's call had given me a rush of excitement, but instead of getting my girlfriend back, I was dealing with the possibility that Royal's gang wanted retribution.

We left Dr. Yushenko's office and got back in my car. I said, "You were lucky. It could have been worse than a mild concussion."

"Getting bopped on the head and missing my pizza isn't exactly what I'd call lucky."

"How are you feeling?"

"Just a headache, but it's not like the one I had with Covid."

"Good. Call Susan. I want her to stay with you."

"I don't feel like entertaining."

"You don't have to. She needs to keep an eye on you. Don't be a hero. If your memory blanks out or you feel nauseous—"

"Nauseous? I'm starving."

"Order something and get it delivered. But remember, you need to be on the lookout if you feel super tired or become irritable."

"I'm going to be fine, Daddy."

"Don't be a macho man. I need you around, especially if Royal's guys are coming after us."

"I can't figure this out. I thought it was him, but maybe I was wrong. I could have been thrown off after getting whacked."

"You're pretty observant, but either way, we can't take a chance. If they're gunning for us, we need to be prepared."

"It just doesn't make sense; why do it in a public place?"

"The only thing I can think of is the surprise factor. We let our guard down in places like that."

"Maybe it wasn't planned, and Hound saw me and just acted."

"That would never fly if Royal was around. He had too much discipline."

"You're right. Maybe Hound went rogue."

"After I drop you off, I'm going see what I can find out."

Larson opened the door without asking who was there.

"You didn't check to see who it was."

He held up his phone. "I saw it was you."

"You finally hooked up the cameras?"

"Yeah, Harry installed everything in an hour."

"What made you do it now?"

"I don't know. Just got tired of seeing it sitting in the

closet."

Did Larson know something? "I didn't know Harry knew how to do that."

"Oh yeah, he even installed a camera out back."

"Well, I'm glad you finally got it up and running."

"Are you here about Barrone?"

"No. Mario was attacked today."

"Oh no! How is he?"

"Good, he's resting."

"What happened?"

I relayed the events, and Larson said, "You really think it's Royal's guys?"

"I don't know. You hearing anything on their activities?"

"Not a peep."

"What about any infighting?"

"I haven't heard a word."

"What about their operations?"

"As far as I know, nothing has changed. The Rodriguez brothers came down from Orlando after Royal blew himself up, but Royal's crew shut them right down."

"So, nothing changed? They're motoring along?"

"Yeah, speaking of motoring, where are you with the car thing?"

"It's evolving, but the target swallowed the hook."

"Mario told me this one is paying well."

"What else did he say?"

"Nothing, just that you were on a high-end job."

"It pays well, but it's a big production with a ton of expenses."

"How are you doing with the Lombardy case Ventura gave you?"

"Is there anything you don't know?"

He smiled. "It's my job."

And mine. "Mario thinks the injury is legit."

"Really? The doctor he's going to has a history of trumping up injury claims."

"I'll make sure either way."

"We don't have much time. The trial starts in a couple of days."

41

The traffic eased on Route 41 after the Golden Gate Boulevard intersection. Continuing north, I spotted the Hampton Inn and turned right. A block before Goodlette Frank Road, I parked across the street from Munoz's house.

Munoz wasn't much of a painter; his drab green house was thirsting for a coat of paint. There looked to be an hour of daylight left. The white Ford Edge registered to Munoz sat in his driveway.

I got out of my car and opened the hood. Bending over the engine, I waited a minute before approaching Munoz's house. Keeping my eyes on the front window, I hit the bell. Past the empty family room, a slice of the kitchen was visible.

Hands on his neck brace, Munoz came into view. A second later the door swung open. "What do you want?"

"I hate to ask, but"—I hiked a thumb at my car—"my car is dead. You think you can give me a jump."

"You got cables?"

"No."

He pointed to a house a couple of doors down. "Try Franco, he's got a garage full of tools."

"Okay, thanks. If I can't get it started, I'll have to leave it overnight and get it towed in the morning. Can you keep an eye on it for me?"

He shrugged. "I'm leaving at seven, but it'll be okay out there."

"Thanks, man."

I went to the house Munoz suggested and made like I'd rung the wrong bell. As dusk drew its curtains, I climbed into my car. Under the cover of darkness, I'd implement my plan and call an Uber.

The next morning, Mario picked me up, and we went back to Munoz's to get my car. I checked the video from the dash cam I had set up. It was golden. We faked jump-starting my car and went our separate ways.

I went home, swapped cars, and drove Larson's Ferrari to Caden's house. It took a while, but Caden answered the door holding a mug of coffee. He squinted his eyes. I asked, "What's the matter? Too early for you?"

He grunted, turning back into the house.

I said, "Late night?"

"Too much tequila."

"Where'd you go?"

"Who remembers? We started at Good Times, then it was Mr. Tequila, and who knows where else."

"Guess you were driving the Maserati last night."

He poured another cup of coffee. "I had to close one eye to get home."

"You should be careful."

"I am. I know how to drive when I'm partying."

"It only takes a second, and things spin out of control."

"What did you want?"

"Remember I told you about getting another Ferrari?"

"Yeah, you wanted the low-end one."

"I liked the Roma."

Caden put his cup down and dug out a vial of coke. "You want a bump?"

"No."

Caden closed a nostril with a finger and snorted a spoonful. He shook his head and rubbed his nose. "That's better. Look, if you're going to get a Roma, don't waste your time. It's a starter model."

"I think it's nice."

"Be a man and upgrade or stick with the Portofino."

"I have to think it over. It's a ton of dough."

"It's only money." He snorted another spoonful.

"I know, but I didn't do as well as you did."

"Not many people did. I did what I had to do to make it. It's all there for the taking, if you want it."

Not many people were the only child of a wealthy father. "You make it seem easy."

"For me it is."

"So, what model do you think I should consider? But nothing crazy expensive."

"Why don't we take a ride to the dealership tomorrow? I'll talk to Dino, see what kind of deal he can make for you."

"Really? Man, I appreciate it."

"Those motherfuckers owe me. It's their fault my Aperta is gone. I got a bad feeling they were in on it."

"The Ferrari dealer?"

"There's no doubt about it."

"Are you sure?"

"How else could it have happened? I think that fuck Freddo

has something going on with the guineas in Italy. It's probably a Mafia thing."

"I guess they could be. Have you heard of something like this happening before?"

"Happens all the time. Even Jerry Seinfeld got scammed."

"Really?"

"Yep, he bought what he thought was a Porsche and it turned out to be a fake."

"A fake Porsche?"

"Yeah, he paid, like, two million for a 1958 Porsche 356A Carrera, and it turned out to be a fake."

"Wow, I didn't know. Maybe I should reconsider buying one."

"Don't wait, man. They only get more expensive as time goes by."

"I know, but I'm not quite ready to buy. I have a real estate investment that I'm unwinding. It'll take a month or two to wrap up."

"That's okay. You'll get an idea of what's out there. A lot of times, there's just no inventory, and you have to look at something gently used."

"You have to be careful with used ones; people abuse these cars. I never would have bought mine if it wasn't my friend's."

"Don't worry, I'll know everything about anything for sale."

He knew it all. They should put Caden to work finding a cure for cancer. "All right, I'll see you tomorrow."

Larson wanted to talk. I left Caden's home, and a minute later I pulled into the garage for Vanderbilt Beach. Cabana Dan gave me a warm smile and pointed to the southern end of the beach.

It was another in a long line of perfect days. Careful not to get sand in my sneakers, I trudged along the vegetation berm to Larson's regular spot.

Perched on the edge of a chaise, Larson was on the phone. He threw up a hand, and as I slid onto a chair, he hung up. "What a day. Look at the water."

"It's like a lake."

"Do you know what you're looking at? The view, it hasn't changed in thousands of years. Think about that. It's amazing, isn't it?"

I said, "Wait till they start putting those wind generators out there."

"Not in Florida, at least not in my lifetime."

"I wouldn't be so sure about that. The feds are pushing their agenda, and with the thousands of miles of coastline we have, they're going to shove it down our throats. They have it in for Florida."

"It'd be a battle, and whoever is forcing it can forget about getting the state's voters to go for them."

"If they could put them far enough away, so you couldn't see them—"

"That will be the line the politicians sell it on. Then it'll be, well, there was a problem and this and that, and next thing you know, the view will be lost, forever."

"They should pass some laws, now, to prevent it."

"That only protects us for a couple of miles. After that, it's under the feds' jurisdiction."

"But someone six feet tall can see just to three miles. Something could be worked out."

"You have more faith in the federal government than I do, Beck."

"Maybe it's because being ten years younger, I have less experience."

He smiled. "That's definitely it."

"What did you want to talk about?"

He lowered his voice. "I made a couple of inquiries. It looks like Hound was flying solo."

"He acted alone?"

"Looks like it was nothing more than a dick-measuring contest."

"Are you sure about this?"

"I have it from two sources. Apparently, J-Dog and Greezy were challenging a bunch of guys a week ago at Bar X. Believe it or not, they ran a contest. Offering up to twenty thousand to whoever came in first."

"First in what?"

"Attacking someone as sport, like it was some kind of game."

"Are you shitting me?"

"I wish I was, but these guys are as primitive as they come."

"But why Mario?"

"Hound thought he'd score more points on a two-for-one deal."

42

Using Larson's Ferrari, I picked up Caden. Along the short drive to the Ferrari dealership on Tamiami Trail, I said, "I can tell you're feeling better."

"I wasn't sick."

"No, I mean, you know, worried about the call from the prosecutor about the accident."

"It didn't really bother me. I was just surprised, that's all."

"Well, I'm glad it's behind you."

As he nodded, his phone rang. "Hello? Who the fuck is this?" He hung up.

"What's going on?"

"I've been getting these calls. Sometimes they hang up, and a couple of times they say they're coming after me."

Pulling into the parking lot, I said, "Coming after you? Why? What does that even mean?"

He lowered his voice. "They said next time they were going to take more."

"More of what?"

"Got no fucking idea, but I'm putting cameras in my garage

in case they're going after another one of my cars. I can't take another hit like that."

"Stealing a car would be crazy."

Caden stepped out of the car. "People do it all the time."

"I don't know. Are you sure it's not just some kids screwing around?"

"Unfortunately, I'm sure it isn't."

He waved. I looked in that direction, and the general manager, Dino, was standing outside smoking.

Caden shook his hand. "Dino, how's it hanging?"

"Good to see you, Mr. Beck."

Inhaling the cigarette smoke felt good. "Same here, it's just Beck though."

"Yeah, he's like Bono, uses just one name."

"Give me your key. I'll have it washed while you're here."

I put the fob in Dino's extended hand. "Thanks."

Dino handed off the key and snuffed out the cigarette in a standing tray. He opened the door. "Come in, gentlemen."

The showroom was cool and smelled like a spa. An entirely new selection of cars was on the floor.

Caden said, "I like the new yellow paint on the 812 GTS."

Dino said, "We didn't make any changes."

"No way. That's a shade richer."

"It could be the light."

We followed Caden to the car. He bent down. "I think they added another couple of layers. It almost has a translucent look to it."

"Perhaps. Mr. Caden said you're interested in a new Ferrari."

"I'm thinking about it."

"What price range are you considering?"

Caden, who had his head in the yellow vehicle, said, "He should get an 812. I love it in Rosso Corsa."

A man in jeans hovered nearby. Caden studied the man and whispered, “Who is that?”

Dino said, “I don’t know. He came in right behind us.”

I said, “Do you have an 812 in red?”

“It’s sold already, but we can take a look at it. It’s being prepped for delivery.”

“How long is delivery time?”

“I’m sorry, but we’re not taking any more orders for the 812 GTS. You’d have to choose something out of inventory.”

“Oh, that’s too bad. I’d like to see the red one anyway.”

“Absolutely. Let’s go to the prep area.”

We followed Dino, and Caden whispered, “That guy is right behind us.”

“He probably just wants to see the car as well.”

“I don’t like the way he’s looking at me.”

“Relax, Brett. It’s nothing.”

Dino held the door open, and we entered the prep and delivery area. It was hospital clean. The throaty rumble of a car being serviced in the adjoining garage was the perfect soundtrack.

Dino pointed to two men wiping a car with sheepskin cloths. “There she is. It’s a beauty, isn’t it?”

It stopped me in my tracks. I wasn’t a car guy, but for how much longer was the question. We circled the vehicle. It bordered on breathtaking. Caden asked, “What is it going for?”

“Just under five hundred.”

The half-a-million price tag crushed my budding dream of owning one.

“It’ll be worth six before the year is out.”

Dino noticed the other man and asked, “Can I assist you with anything?”

He wagged his head and went back into the showroom.

Dino said, "We have another 812 on the upper floor. It's a magnificent Bianco Cervino."

Caden said, "It's the most gorgeous white that Ferrari has ever done."

"Let's take a look."

We took the elevator and, stepping out, Dino got a call on his cell. Caden and I circled the white sports car. Caden whispered, "I didn't like that guy downstairs. He didn't say a word."

"You're making something out of nothing."

"Who the hell is he?"

"You're imagining things."

"Yeah?" He threw a chin, and I followed it. The man worrying Caden was at the top of the stairs of our floor, looking in our direction.

43

Caden said, "Let's get out of here."

Dino said, "Is everything all right?"

Caden headed to the elevator. "Come on. Let's go."

I said, "His stomach was bothering him. I told him we could come another day, but he pushed himself."

"I hope he feels better."

"Thanks, Dino. Let me think about a car. I don't have the resources other buyers have, and it's a big commitment for me."

"I understand completely. Take your time. I'm available to help whenever you're ready."

Caden was leaving the showroom when I caught up with him. "Hey, hang on."

We stepped into the parking lot. Caden looked up. "That bastard is watching me."

"I don't know that he is."

"Come on, man. What, are you blind? He's been following us since we got here."

"Who do you think it could be?"

"I don't know. You think he could be an undercover cop?"

"An undercover cop? Why would they—"

"You forget about the prosecutor who called me?"

"Oh yeah, I guess it's possible."

"I don't like the way this feels."

Engine purring, a midnight-blue Ferrari pulled into a spot. I said, "Hey, it's Bob Stone. You remember him from the rally. We sat at the same table at Barbatella."

Caden scoffed, "Pompous ass thinks his bullshit McLaren is the fastest thing on earth."

"He knows a lot about cars."

"Not more than me."

Stone got out and I walked over. "Hey, Bobby. What's going on?"

"Beck. You buy something yet?"

"Still trying to decide. We saw a nice GTS."

"The white one upstairs?"

"Yeah, it's pretty, isn't it?"

He nodded. "Is that your friend?"

"Yeah." I called out, "Brett, come say hello."

Caden trudged over. "Hey, Bob Stone, right?"

"Yep, how are you, uh—"

"Brett, Brett Caden."

"Oh yeah, sorry, man. Now I remember. You thought your 788 GTS was faster than my 720S."

"It is."

Stone laughed. "Yeah, if that's what you want to believe, go for it."

"It has nothing to do with belief, it's a proven fact."

"I don't know where you get your facts from, but everybody knows a McLaren 720S is faster than a 788 GTS."

"It is not."

"It is!"

"It fucking isn't."

I said, "Take it easy, boys."

Stone said, "Beck is right. We should tone it down."

Caden said, "Even if your shitty McLaren was fast enough to beat my GTS, it depends on the driver."

"True. I'm no pro, but I've been on enough tracks to hold my own. How about you?"

"I've done more than my fair share of racing and never lost a race yet."

"Doing a little bit of bragging, huh?"

"It ain't bragging if it's true."

"We're not talking about the kiddy track, are we?"

"Fuck you."

I said, "Guys, be nice."

Caden said, "Let's get out of here."

Stone said, "Anytime you want to race, just let Beck know. That is, if you're not afraid."

I said, "We'll see you around, Bobby."

We climbed into Larson's Ferrari. Caden said, "What the fuck is wrong with that guy?"

"Bobby is good people. He's just a bit full of himself when it comes to cars. Tell you the truth, I saw him race a couple of times at the Lamborghini thing. He didn't impress me."

"He needs to shut his mouth."

"You know, I don't know anything about racing, but the last time we went to Miami Speedway, he barely made the first qualifying round, and then the second round kicks off, and he's way behind. Next thing I know, after the third lap, he drops out and pulls into the pit."

"Chickenshit."

"Bobby said it was something mechanical, but another of my buddies, who knows, said that was an excuse."

"He's got some balls running his mouth off."

"You should take him up on the challenge."

"Race him?"

"Why not? I'd pay to see how he explains it when you leave him in the dust."

Caden shrugged. "These races aren't blowouts. You beat a high-end machine by a car length, it's a runaway."

"Whatever. If you can beat him, he'll have to shut up."

"If? I know I would."

"So, let's do it, then."

"It's not easy getting a track to do it on."

"You said Lamborghini did something with the Miami Speedway."

"They do."

"You know the people at Lamborghini. Can't you get them to help?"

"They don't want to get involved in a private thing; they want to showcase their own cars."

"There's got to be a place."

As we pulled in front of Caden's house, his phone rang. "Hello? Hello? Who is this?" Leave me the fuck alone!"

Caden shoved his phone in a pocket, and I asked, "Who was that?"

"It's got to be the same guys."

I revved the engine several times before shutting it down. "What guys?"

"If I knew, I'd fucking tell you."

I pointed at a man in a cap and full beard who was walking along the side of Caden's house. "Who's that?"

Caden froze before saying, "Hey! What the hell are you doing?"

The man looked our way. "Nothing, just checking the view out back."

"Get the hell out of here."

The guy got into his car and drove away. Caden said, "You see? I'm not losing it."

"We should check out the back of the house."

"You think he was trying to get in?"

"You never know."

Caden went straight to the garage. He punched in the code, and as the door rolled up, he bent down. "They're all here."

"Good. Go through the house. I'll check around back."

Caden stepped onto his deck. Standing on the dock below, I said, "You're going to want to see this."

"What? What's wrong?"

44

As soon as I got home, my phone rang, it was Caden. "Hey, Brett, how are you doing?"

"Terrible. Did you see this shit about Puzo?"

I knew all about it. "No. What's going on?"

"The sleazebag made some kind of a deal and was released."

"Really?"

"Yeah, and he took off for Italy."

"Italy?"

"Yeah, they said he rented a house on Lake Como."

"He has the money to—"

"He's hiding out like the rat he is."

"Puzo might have spilled the beans on a couple of his clients."

"I don't give a shit about any of them but what he said about me."

"I know. Larson said he told you—"

"He had to be the one to leave the newspaper article."

"The one I found in your backyard?"

"Yep, there is no doubt in my mind."

"Because it was about the accident?"

There was a pause as he snorted a line. "Yeah, he kept, like, a frigging scrapbook of every article and news report on the accident."

Puzo always did. "He did?"

"Yeah, he said it was to make sure he had proof of an unfair trial if we lost. But I know that's bullshit now; he wanted stuff to use against me."

"I don't know about that."

"Yeah? Well, I do. Who else would dredge all this up?"

"You got a point."

"They're coming after me."

"Take it easy. Remember, you're protected by double jeopardy."

"I'm sure there's something else Puzo cooked up. I mean, he knows everything and . . . I'm screwed. I can feel it."

"Relax. You know, I have a lot of contacts."

"I'm betting Puzo told the Peterson family everything."

"Yeah, that's possible. I didn't think of that. What could he have said?"

"They're coming after me. What am I going to do?"

"You got to calm down."

"I can't."

"You have to. Take five deep breaths through your nose, and exhale slowly out of your mouth."

Caden sucked in air and released it as instructed. I said, "Feel better?"

"I don't know."

"Look, hang in there. I have to run an errand; I'll call you in an hour."

"Can you come over?"

"Let me see how it goes. I'll let you know."

I hung up. "Come on, Toby. We're going for a walk."

Toby raised his head. When I grabbed his leash, he leapt out of his bed.

After walking a block, Toby slowed down. He sniffed, looking for the perfect spot to leave his mark, and I took a burner phone out. I tapped in a number and Caden answered: "Hello?"

I remained silent.

"Hello?"

"Hey! Who the fuck is this?"

I hung up.

Toby did his business, and we went back into the house. I grabbed another burner, and using a voice distortion app, called Caden again.

He answered but said nothing for a couple of seconds. "Hello?"

"You better watch your back, buddy."

"Who is this?"

"We're coming after you."

"Fuck you!"

"We're finally going to get you."

Caden hung up.

I put a load of wash on and made a sandwich. Searching for a podcast Larson had told me about, my phone rang. It was Caden.

"Beck! Beck! I don't know what's wrong with me."

"What's the matter?"

"I can't breathe. And my chest has all this pressure on it."

"Maybe it's a heart attack."

"What?"

"Any pain or feeling of numbness in your left arm?"

"No."

"How bad is the pressure?"

"Not so bad, but something is going on."

"Sit tight. I'll run right over."

Caden's shirt was darkened with sweat. "How are you feeling?"

His breathing was a tick away from hyperventilation. "Not good . . . not good."

"Lay down on the couch."

I grabbed a water bottle out of the refrigerator. "Sip this."

"My heart is pounding."

"How about your hands? Feeling anything?"

"Tingly."

"When did all this start happening?"

"After I talked to you, I got a couple of calls from them."

"Who?"

"The people after me."

"What people?"

"If I fucking knew who they were, I'd tell you!"

"Take it easy. What did they say?"

"They were coming after me. They were gonna finally get me."

"And that's what started what you're feeling?"

He nodded and wiped his forehead with his sleeve.

"You're having a panic attack. Did you ever have one before?"

"No!"

"Relax and lay off the coke."

"I hardly did any today."

"Are you feeling any better?"

"A little."

"All right. I have to get back to work. I'll check on you later."

45

I sat in my car waiting. As soon as it hit 1:00 p.m., I headed to the courtroom. Ventura had called; the plaintiff had rested his case. Ventura was going to begin defending his client after a brief recess for lunch.

The prudent thing to do was to maintain a low profile, but it wasn't just the money that motivated me. Limping through the metal detector, the guard didn't recognize me. The pair of glasses, facial hair, ball cap, and arm crutch were effective.

There were a handful of people in the courtroom. As Rigo Munoz was being reminded he was still under oath, I took a seat in the second-to-last pew.

Phil Ventura approached the witness stand. "Mr. Munoz, that neck brace seems uncomfortable."

"It sure is."

"I'm sorry to have to bring you back to the stand. Are you ready to continue?"

Munoz grimaced. "I'm in a lot of pain, but I just want to get this over with."

"I'll do my best to move things along. You've previously

testified you suffered several debilitating injuries from a fall at Mr. Puglia's home."

"I did."

"I don't want to get this wrong and minimize what happened to you. Would you please remind the court of the injuries?"

"I have a lot of nerve damage. My back and neck are in constant pain, and the retina in my left eye was partial detached."

"It's my understanding that the retina has fully recovered. Is that accurate?"

"Yes."

"I thought so. Our optometrist couldn't find any evidence it was detached."

Munoz's lawyer said, "Objection. Our experts testified regarding the detachment. Nine months have passed since hazardous conditions caused Mr. Munoz to fall."

"Sustained."

"How is your vision now?"

"Still blurry."

"Even though it's healed?"

"The doctors say it will take a long time and may never recover fully."

"I'm not a physician, but I think you'll be fine. Now, how did you fall?"

"I was on a ladder, painting the crown molding. And the next thing I remember, I was falling. I hit the floor. It's marble, and I blacked out."

"How long were you unconscious?"

"I don't know, maybe five minutes."

"Did you hit your head?"

"No, I don't think so."

"Did you get a concussion?"

"Not that I know of, but it's possible."

"How did you lose consciousness if you didn't hit your head?"

"Objection. Mr. Munoz is not a medical professional and is not qualified to answer."

"Sustained."

"Are you in pain all the time, Mr. Munoz?"

"Yes, it never ends."

"I can't imagine that. All day, you're in pain?"

"Yes."

"And your neck, it hurts?"

"It's terrible. I can't describe it."

"You have to wear that brace all the time?"

"Yes."

"Even when sleeping?"

"Yes."

"You never take it off?"

"No. The doctors say I could become paralyzed if I do."

"That sounds scary."

"It is. I'm so afraid I'll be in a wheelchair the rest of my life."

"I imagine you'd be extra careful as to what your day-to-day activities are."

"I'm in too much pain to do anything. All I do is watch TV. The only time I leave my house is to go see doctors."

"I'm sorry to hear that. You testified earlier that the doctors said you were at risk of being paralyzed. Did they give you any specifics on what to avoid doing?"

"They don't want me to bend down unless it's necessary."

"How about lifting things?"

"They strictly forbid lifting anything. Besides, just picking up a cup of coffee is painful."

Ventura turned to the jury. "We certainly sympathize with

the type of pain and life-altering injuries Mr. Munoz described. If that harm was caused by negligence, a willful and total disregard for the injured person's safety, then it's reasonable awarding compensation, as a form of making amends, would be justified."

The jury box was a sea of nodding heads as Ventura said, "Before we attempt to calculate what dollar amount is fair, I'd like to play a video."

A monitor was rolled out.

"Please pay close attention to this film. I believe a reasonable person would know it contains all you need to make the proper judgment in this case."

Ventura was handed the remote, and the entire box of jurors leaned forward.

"As you can see, the time stamp is seven forty-five on the morning of May second. The house pictured is owned by Mr. Munoz."

Ventura zoomed in. "That's Mr. Munoz exiting the home. He's wearing the neck brace he has on now."

As Munoz skipped down the steps to the driveway, Ventura said, "I'm no doctor, but he seems to be moving pretty quickly to me."

Munoz stopped and bent over, looking at the passenger front tire. "Looks like he has a flat."

Munoz shook his head and surveyed the street before going to the trunk. The lid of the trunk opened, and he bent over, pulling out a jack and lug wrench.

Ventura smiled. "I hope those don't weigh too much."

Munoz set them down by the front of the car and put his hands to his neck. Ventura paused the video, saying, "You can clearly see, Mr. Munoz is taking his neck brace off."

"Objection." Munoz's lawyer shot out of his seat. "The court cannot allow this to be played until we can verify its authenticity. For all we know, it can be a deepfake made with AI."

"Overruled. You'll have an opportunity to examine the video. We'll allow it."

Venture smiled and resumed playing the tape.

"He's changing the tire. Anyone who has changed one knows that the amount of force needed to loosen a lug is substantial."

Ventura froze the video as Munoz put one end of the wrench on the lug and grabbed the lever part. "I know it may sound convenient, but about six years ago, I got a flat on Santa Barbara Boulevard and threw my back out trying to get a lug off." He put his hand on his hip and frowned. "Let's watch the rest of this."

Munoz took off the lugs and grabbed the wheel with both hands, pulling it off the car. He rolled it, leaning it against his vehicle. He picked up the spare and bent down, maneuvering it onto the car.

Ventura said, "I don't know about you, but most people would say Munoz looks completely healthy to me. He hasn't stopped to rest and is moving fluidly."

The lawyer paused, making eye contact with each juror before saying, "I'm not a doctor, but I wasn't born yesterday either. I believe Mr. Munoz has been caught red-handed trying to scam a settlement from Mr. Puglia."

46

Getting someone's cell phone number wasn't a challenge. I popped Dr. Schwartz's number into a burner phone. It rang five times before going to voice mail.

"Hey, Doc, give me a call. I have something I don't think you'd want your wife to see."

It took a minute before a text pinged: *Who is this?*

A friend. Call me. Now.

The phone rang. It was the podiatrist. "Hey, Doc, we have to meet."

"Who is this?"

"Consider me a friend. I have something you definitely wouldn't want your wife to see."

"What are you talking about?"

"Tight white pants—ring a bell?"

"I don't have any idea what you're referring to."

"Does the Marriott TownePlace hotel help you?"

He hesitated. "What do you want, money?"

"No. I'm just trying to help everybody out. Let's meet up."

Another long pause. "I don't like this. Are you Janet's husband? Are you going to hurt me?"

Great. We had two cheaters. “Take it easy. I’m not going to lay a finger on you. Let’s get together, and I’ll explain everything.”

“Where? It’s got to be a public place.”

“Sure. How about Waterside Shops?”

Three beats passed before he said, “Okay. What time?”

It was supposed to start raining in ninety minutes. “Two hours from now.”

“All right. Where?”

“How about by the parking garage.”

“Okay.”

“Don’t be late. I hate it when people are late.”

47

The late-lunch crowd was long gone at Seasons 52. I was the only one sitting at the bar. Ventura settled onto a stool. "I don't know how you do it."

"I can't give away secrets."

"Always guarded, aren't you?"

"That was a good move, not sharing it with the defense. They would have folded before the trial, and we wouldn't have gotten a show."

"Judge Wilkins wasn't happy about it. He was making noise about going after Munoz for perjury."

"It's too murky when someone claims nerve damage. But he'll never do something like that again."

"Exactly. And with the press getting ahold of it, nobody will try to go after Puglia again." Ventura handed me an envelope. "Puglia was so grateful, he added a little something as a bonus."

I opened the envelope. The check was for three hundred thousand. "An extra fifty is a little something?"

"Puglia said it was worth the show."

"I just shot the video. You added the drama, ratcheting up the tension before cutting Munoz down."

"You were smart enough to film it, but that was some stroke of luck that Munoz had a flat."

I smiled.

"You didn't puncture his tire, did you?"

There was no need to lie. "Of course not." Puncturing a tire would have left a trail, putting Munoz on guard. Letting the air out of the valve was untraceable.

48

I PARKED BY THE APPLE STORE AND WALKED UNDER THE overhangs of Waterside Shops. It was near closing time. The only place busy was BrickTop's. The rain had killed Bravo's bar and outdoor dining business.

I waited just inside the quarter-full parking garage. A few shoppers scurried into the lot and left the mall.

It was easy to spot Schwartz before I could see his face. Carrying an umbrella, his head swiveled from side to side. I stepped from behind the column and put a hand up. About to cross the street, the podiatrist stopped in his tracks. He scanned the area and approached slowly. I slipped behind the column.

He paused at the entrance. I pointed to the ramp leading to the second floor and started up it.

"Hey, hold on a second."

I turned around. "Keep quiet and start walking, or your wife isn't going to be happy with you."

"I'm not going anywhere. Just what do you think you're doing?"

Pulling my phone out, I walked toward the foot doctor. I

shoved the screen in his face. “You see this? Looks an awful lot like you, doesn’t it?”

“Where’d you get that? You were following me?”

“Shut up and get moving.” I turned around and kept climbing to the second floor. Hearing another set of footsteps meant Schwartz was following.

There were no cars on the second floor of the garage. I walked to the far corner and watched Schwartz trudge over.

An SUV came down from the rooftop. I ducked behind a pillar until it passed. It was the last vehicle up there. Schwartz stopped a car length away. “You going to tell me what the hell this is about?”

“Watch your temper. You’re in no position to ask questions.”

“What do you want from me? Money?”

“Come here.”

I played the video of him and the woman at the Marriott.

“So, I screwed around a little. It’s no big deal.”

“It’ll be a big deal to your wife, won’t it? And what about her husband?”

He shrugged.

“If you do what I say, I’ll delete the video. If not, I’ll send it to your wife, her father, and the woman’s husband. Your father-in-law will probably cut you right out of any inheritance, and he’s got a lot of money, doesn’t he?”

Another shrug.

“You have a prenup, don’t you?”

He nodded. “Look, you’re taking this too far.”

“And the house is in your wife’s name—”

“Come on. I’m a good person who just made a mistake.”

I scoffed, “Good person? Come on, now.”

“Really, I am.”

“You make a living helping people scam others.”

"What? I don't understand."

"Stress fracture."

"What?"

"You heard me."

"What does a stress fracture have to do with anything?"

"It's why you're here. You and your scumbag lawyer friends use them to fool people."

"No, that's not true."

I threw up a hand. "Don't tell me that. I came to see you myself."

He frowned. "It's not something I do often. Really, you have to believe me."

"Here's what's going to happen. I'm going to send this to your wife, father-in-law, and the *Naples Daily News* if you don't do what I say."

"What? What? You'll ruin my life. I'll do anything."

I looked over the edge. "Jump from here."

"What? That's crazy."

"It's not that high. You might break a leg, but you'll definitely get stress fractures in both legs."

"You got to be kidding me. I'm not jumping."

I pulled my phone out. "Your wife's number is 239-332-4349, right?"

"Who the hell are you?"

"Never mind. Get up there."

"No fucking way."

I pulled out my Glock. "Hurry up. I have another appointment."

"Come on. Please. I'll do anything. I can get money. How much do you want, a hundred thousand, two?"

"Money can't fix everything." I pointed the gun at his leg. "Get up there and jump before I shoot your kneecaps off."

Schwartz scrambled onto the top of the wall. "Please. I'm begging you."

I cocked the gun. "Step down to that ledge. It's not as high."

He held on to the wall and lowered himself. The goal wasn't to have him break his legs or sustain a major injury.

"Jump."

"I can't do it."

I leaned over and pressed the nose of the gun to his thigh. The rain pelted my arm. "I'm going to give you three seconds."

"Please. Please."

"Three, two, one."

Schwartz stepped off. He screamed when he hit the ground. But he scrambled, clutching his legs. I didn't have to dial 9-1-1. I headed out. Schwartz would know what a fracture felt like, and I doubted he'd engage in any more shenanigans.

49

WALKING IN BETWEEN CADEN AND BOB STONE, WE HEADED out of Immokalee Airport's general aviation building. I said, "Looks like they recently renovated this place."

Stone said, "Yeah, a year ago they put the new metal roof on and painted it white."

"It looks good, doesn't it, Brett?"

"It's okay."

A pair of five-hundred-gallon white fuel tanks lined the fence. We crossed a grassy area and hit the tarmac. The heat radiating off the cement warmed my lower legs. Stone bent down and touched the concrete surface. "It's hot, but the sun isn't direct anymore. It'll be fine."

"For what they charged to rent this, you can't expect air-conditioning."

Caden said, "They're making money, or they wouldn't do it."

"You're right, but they had to shut down air traffic, supplied an ambulance, and were cool with us putting together a track rather than just using the drag-racing strip."

Caden said, “Turns and curves are where a driver makes the difference. A dog can drag race.”

“You say that because you know my McLaren will bury anything you own on a drag strip.”

Caden scoffed, “You’ll probably fuck up on the straightaways.”

I said, “We’ll get to settle this in a little while, so hold the trash talk.”

“Just trying to help your delusional buddy.”

I said, “You think drug runners used this airport back in the day?”

Stone said, “Probably, but I can tell you, Naples grows anymore, this airport is going to be worth a hundred times what it is today.”

Caden said, “Naples Airport is way too busy. A private jet is taking off every five minutes, especially in season. They should limit what goes on there.”

Stone replied, “The jet-set image of Naples Airport is not the entire picture. I mean, no doubt the rich use it, but don’t forget the medical helicopters for the area are based there, and the police have their aviation force based there, not to mention the county’s mosquito control operations.”

Caden said, “You wait and see, anything good there is gonna be forced out by the heavy hitters with their private jets.”

Stone pointed. “Are those kids out there?”

Four boys had knocked over one of the orange barrels outlining the turns in the racecourse. I said, “Yeah, they were here when I came last week, playing soccer.”

Caden said, “They shouldn’t be here.”

“The aviation manager said they’re from the area. They use the outer field to kick around a ball.”

“Make sure they stay out of the way.”

"Don't worry, before we kick it off, they'll be off the property."

Stone said, "You know this makeshift track is short. You got a built-in handicap."

"Fuck you."

"I'm serious. You even said my McLaren is faster—"

"Look, man, I'm going to beat your ass so bad, it wouldn't matter if we were racing at Daytona."

"Yeah, right."

"Okay, guys, save it for the track."

Stone said, "Greg is coming with his video setup. He's going to record the finish."

"He's the one who shot the picture in your office?"

"Yep. Hey, Caden, you may want to wear a disguise or something."

"Keep talking, asshole."

I said, "Brett, you said you put new tires on. What kind?"

"Pirelli Prestige."

"You want to show me? I need to learn more about them if I'm going to get another Ferrari. We'll see you later, Bob."

Stone walked away. "You bet."

Caden said, "Hey, Stone! You interested in laying down a wager on the race?"

"Absolutely. But you still have money after you got scammed out of your Aperta?"

Caden face reddened. "More than you'll ever have."

"How about a hundred thousand?"

I said, "Hold on, guys, that's crazy."

"You're on."

Stone said, "I want it in writing."

"You don't trust me?"

"No way."

"Fuck you. Forget it, then."

"See? You had no intention of paying when you lost."

I stepped in front of Caden. "Forget about him. Show me the tires."

His jaw was clenched so tight that his chin quivered. "Motherfucker needs to be smacked down."

"Just beat him and he'll shrink away."

"I'm going to obliterate the bastard."

"I know you will. Just do me a favor and stay away from him. Okay?"

"Yeah, okay."

We had an hour before the flag would go down, a long sixty minutes keeping Caden from getting physical with Stone.

Caden headed to the aviation building. "I gotta take a piss."

Caden ducked into the men's room. A half a minute later, I felt the urge and followed him. Caden was bent over the vanity snorting a line of coke with a rolled-up hundred-dollar bill.

He rubbed his nose. "You want a bump?"

"Not now. I'll wait until you win, then we'll celebrate."

He spilled out another line. "I'm gonna blow his ass away so bad, he'll never race again."

"All you have to do is win. Nobody will remember by how much."

"I will, and so will Stone. I don't want to beat him; I want to annihilate him."

As I stood in front of a urinal, Caden turned the faucet on, wet his fore and middle fingers and inhaled droplets of water. He wanted every last granule of coke.

He left the restroom, and I washed my hands. I was about to exit when the door swung open. It was Caden.

"You forgot to pee?"

"I think the guy that was at my house is here."

"Can't be."

"Check. He's got yellow shorts on and is standing by the counter."

I cracked open the door and looked. "Yeah, you're right. I think it's him."

A drop of sweat fell from the tip of Caden's nose. "Who the fuck is he?"

I shook my head.

"What do you think he wants from me?"

"I don't know. You need to concentrate on the race. Don't let this guy distract you."

"But who is he?"

I looked outside. "He's gone. Let's get out of here. We can't stay in the men's room forever."

"Hold on. I got a fucking headache." He tipped a glassine envelope over and tapped out a small mound.

"You sure that's going to help a headache?"

He used a credit card to make a line, licked the edge, and put it away. He rolled a bill and the powder disappeared up his nose.

"Come on. Let's get to the starting area."

We stepped outside. Caden's head moved birdlike. "You see him?"

"No. He's gone."

"I see him again. I'm going right up to him."

"Forget him for now! You got a race to run." I faced him, putting my hands on his shoulders. "You have to focus, man."

"I will. I'm gonna whip Stone's ass."

I raised a fist. "Let's do it!"

He bumped my fist. "Damn right."

"Look at your car. It looks amazing."

"Who is this guy you got to drop the flag?"

"Ronnie. You never met him?"

"No. Can we trust him to be fair when he starts the race?"

"Definitely. He's a good guy."

"You know, I checked around, and your buddy Stone has a history of cheating."

"Really? How'd he lose in Miami, then?"

"I don't know. Maybe the other guy was a better cheater. You know people cheat all the time."

If you drove a yellow car, you'd notice yellow cars more than the next guy. "It's going to be fair. If something happens, I'll make sure we start over."

"I don't trust Stone; he'll find a way to jump the start."

"It's a ten-lap race, even if he gets a one-second head start, you'll make it up."

"Every second counts. At a hundred miles an hour, a car travels a hundred and fifty feet in a second."

That was more than I expected. "It's going to be okay. Stop worrying. Who knows, you might get off the line before him."

"I gotta take another piss."

"All right, I have to make a call."

As Caden left to snort more cocaine, I checked my phone. Mario still wasn't here and hadn't left a message. I called him again and left another voice mail. We had enough manpower, but this was an important job, and there wasn't room for error.

I had looked out for Mario while in foster care. He used to tell me he didn't want me to watch over him, that he could take care of himself and always threw up the fact he secured the fake IDs we needed to run away. But now he depended on me for work, and when I had to keep him in line from time to time, he never complained. Had the burden of being forced to be responsible as a young boy boomeranged?

His girlfriend, Susan, would know where he was. I didn't have her number, but Laura did. I hesitated before calling my ex, going over what to say to be sure she didn't think I was using it as an excuse to call her. Or was I?

"Laura? It's Beck."

"Oh. Hi."

"How are—?"

"Good. You?"

What was with the one-word answers? "Everything is good. I'm trying to get ahold of Mario, but he's not answering his phone, and I knew you had Susan's number."

"You want me to call her? See what she knows?"

It would get me a second conversation with her. "Sure, that would be great. I appreciate it. So, you've been doing okay?"

"Yes. We've been really busy at work, and my mother came into town."

Hopefully that didn't leave time for a social life. "That's good. Say hello. Don't work too much. You know they say, all work and no play can make you boring."

I regretted it as soon as it tumbled out of my mouth. She didn't say anything, and I tried to recover with, "But you don't have to worry about that."

"Let me call Susan and see what she says."

"Okay, thanks. I really appreciate it."

I played back the conversation. I'd screwed it up. Again. Caden tugged at my arm, whispering, "Who is that guy in black?"

"What guy?"

"By my car. I've been watching him. He better not fuck with my car."

"That's Angelo. He's a neighbor of mine. He's into cars. I told him about this, and he came down."

"I don't want people crowding around me."

The number of people witnessing the race would only make a crowd in a plane's bathroom. "Don't be so jumpy."

"I'm not jumpy. Why are you saying that?"

"It's just a phrase."

"Don't say shit like that."

My phone buzzed. "Hey, Laura. Did you have any luck?"

"Yeah, I spoke to Susan, and she hasn't heard from Mario either."

"Damn."

"She said he left the house around nine to go to the gym and run some errands but never came back."

My phone said it was almost six. "Why didn't she call anybody?"

"I don't know. Maybe because she wasn't feeling good. She has a fever and has been in bed most of the day."

"Where the hell is he?"

"Don't push the panic button yet. It's probably nothing. He's probably drunk in some bar."

He did like his booze. "I doubt it. He was supposed to meet up with me."

"Where was he supposed to meet you?"

"We're working on something."

She hesitated before asking, "Where?"

If I shut her down, I'd never get back with her. "In Fort Myers, off of Daniels Parkway."

"What are you doing there?"

"Meeting with a client."

"What kind of client?"

She was pushing my buttons. "A guy wants to build a commercial building and needs help with some zoning issues."

"You never said you know anything about that kind of thing."

I never said much of anything to her. "I have a lot of contacts that might be useful to him."

"What kind of contacts?"

"Lawyers and such. Look, my client just pulled up. I'll call you later. If you hear from Susan, let me know."

She was playing me, testing to see how far I'd go before shutting down.

I took a handful of pictures, documenting the people at the race, and walked over to Caden. He was kneeling, inspecting a tire.

I asked, "Everything all right?"

"Just making sure nobody screwed with my tires."

"You see the video setup?"

He nodded and moved to the next wheel. "I'm going to take a couple of practice runs, get used to the track."

"Good idea."

"It's not a pure oval like I'm used to."

"You'll do fine."

"Doing fine is bullshit. I want to cream him."

"You said you have the fastest car and you're a better driver."

"Like Dale Earnhardt Jr. said, 'The winner ain't the one with the fastest car. It's the one who refuses to lose.'"

"That's a good one."

He stood after inspecting the last tire. "And I definitely refuse to lose."

The starter walked over. "Take a few practice laps, then we'll drop the flag."

50

With both cars lined up in front of him, the starter stood between Caden and Stone and said, "Let's have a fair, fun race, gentlemen. First and foremost is safety. Don't put yourself, the other driver, or your vehicles in danger. If there's an incident, we've got an ambulance standing ready." He pointed to the emergency vehicle parked before the far turn. "Let them do their job if something happens. Understood?"

Both drivers nodded.

He continued, "Good. This is a ten-lap event. I'll start by dropping the flag with my right hand. Keep your eyes on my left hand. I'll use my fingers to count down from five before dropping the flag with my right arm. If you're experiencing a mechanical issue, please pull off the track. This is a short race, and you don't have a pit crew to fix whatever might happen. I know both of you want to cross the finish line first, but the main thing is to have fun and drive safely."

Caden and Stone nodded again.

"Okay, gentlemen, let's shake hands and get this started!"

Stone smiled, extending his hand. Caden turned away, walking to his car.

Stone climbed into his McLaren. The last of the sunlight was bouncing off his car's impressive aerodynamics. The gull-wing door lowered, encasing him like an astronaut. The engine came to life, and Stone inched toward the starting line.

My gaze went to Caden's Ferrari. It was a sleek and powerful machine, exuding the confidence its driver lacked. It was as sexy as an inanimate object could hope to be.

Both vehicles were attractive, rolling forms of art.

Caden was circling his car. I trotted over. "Everything okay?"

"It looks like it, but the starter looked at me when mentioning mechanical issues."

"I don't understand."

"I think somebody is monkeying with my car."

"But everything looks good."

"On the outside."

"The cars have been sitting here. If somebody did something, we would have seen them."

He scoffed, "There's a ton of electronics under the hood. It's easier than you think to fuck with them."

"You're right, I never thought about that."

"Nobody believes me anymore."

"I believe you, man. But the reality is, if they did something, you can't do anything about it now."

"I'll get the fuckers if they did."

"Come on. Get in your car. Stone is at the line already."

Caden was in the right-hand lane, and Stone was a couch-length to his left. The starter was standing on a riser. The ear-splitting sound from both drivers revving their engines had me knocking on their windows. Motioning to turn it down, I said, "We're about to kick it off!"

They dialed back the throaty roar, and the starter raised his arm. Heart pounding, I jogged backward down the side of the track.

The race initiator stuck his forefinger up. One. The drivers' weight on their accelerator pedals increased with each raised finger the starter thrust up.

The green flag dropped, and the sports cars exploded off the line with a screech. They surged forward at breathtaking speed, and the smell of burnt rubber filled the air.

Standing on my toes, I tried to see who was in the lead. It was a blur of color with the two of them neck and neck.

Approaching the first turn, the boisterous sound of the engines lessened as they downshifted. Stone lost ground as he floated closer to Caden entering the curve.

The rear of Caden's car drifted within inches of the orange barrels lining the turn.

"Slow down" tumbled out of my mouth as they hit the straightaway. Stone accelerated ahead of Caden as they approached the turn closest to the start and finish line.

Caden's car fishtailed slightly as he catapulted out of the curve into the straightaway, and he had the lead.

As the pair zoomed by, one of the soccer-playing boys came into view. Kicking his ball, he got closer to the track.

Bob Stone's partner shouted, "You got this, Bobby!" He was positioned behind the barrel at the beginning of the turn. Approaching the turn, Caden drifted to the inner side, trying to prevent Stone from catching up.

Stone backed off. Hugging the rear of Caden's Ferrari through the turn, Stone veered to the inside and tapped into the McLaren's s extraordinary power. Looking as if his car was nailed to the pavement, he burst forward, reclaiming the lead by half a car.

The cars maneuvered, playing cat and mouse with the lead

into the next turn. Stone blasted ahead as they took the turn. Caden jockeyed for position as they hit the straightaway.

Stone slowed, approaching the next turn, but Caden didn't let up. My eyes were drawn to the soccer ball. It was arcing in the air, above the track.

Below it, a boy.

A screech.

Caden's car swerved. *Bam!*

He'd hit the boy running after the ball. Both Caden and Stone steered their cars off the track, bouncing onto the grassy area before coming to a stop.

A pair of EMT technicians jumped out of the ambulance. One ran to the boy, and the other ripped open the rear doors, grabbing a gurney. As he wheeled it toward the scene, the tech shouted, "Back away! Make room."

I stretched out my arms. "They need space to work on him. Please stay back."

"How is he?"

The gull wings on Stone's car lifted and he scrambled onto his feet. Caden got out, leaving the door to his Ferrari open. Stone tried to intercept Caden, but he pushed Stone away.

As the paramedics loaded the gurney into the ambulance, I ran toward Caden. "Take it easy! It's going to be okay."

"What the fuck was he doing here?"

"He must have slipped in."

Sirens wailing and lights flashing, the ambulance took off.

51

Caden put his hands on his head. “Where are they taking him?”

“The hospital.”

“Is he gonna be all right?”

I pointed to the blood where the kid had lain. “He was hurt pretty bad.”

“I fucking can’t believe it! I got no luck! None, not a fucking inch of luck.”

“Take it easy; it was an accident.”

Stone walked up. “Jesus Christ, what the hell happened?”

I said, “The kids that were playing soccer before, one of them was running after a ball and—”

“You were going too fast, man.”

“Fuck you. I wasn’t.”

I said, “It looked like you weren’t slowing down for the turn.”

“He jumped out. I didn’t see him. Next thing I knew . . .”

“It’s all right, man. He’ll be on his feet in no time.”

Stone said, “I hate to tell you, buddy, but look at that blood. You creamed the kid.”

Caden's jaw dropped. I squeezed his shoulder. "Take it easy. There's no sense getting worked up."

"But, but—"

"Get in your car and go home. I'll check on the kid and meet you there."

"I can't believe this shit."

I said, "Bob, I don't want word of this getting out. To anyone."

"Don't worry, Beck. Whatever you say."

"And that goes for your people, okay?"

"No worries."

"Make sure of it."

"I will."

"Hang on." I put the phone to my ear, faking a call. "Oh, man! That's great. He's doing good! Thanks." I fake hung up and said, "Tell your guys the boy got up in the ambulance and is on his feet."

"You got it, Beck. Anything else I can do for you?"

"Nothing."

"You sure?"

"Yes. If I need something, I'll let you know."

"Okay, whatever you need."

I put my arm around Caden's shoulder and walked him to his car. "Don't worry, I got this. The kid was hurt bad, but I'll handle this."

"But you said he was okay."

I shook my head. "He's not. I didn't want Stone to know, but I don't think he was breathing."

"Was he conscious?"

"No."

"Oh shit! What if he dies?"

"Let me deal with it."

"Handle what? The kid is going to die. How the fuck you gonna handle that?"

I turned him around, putting my hands on his shoulders. "I have a lot of friends, in and out of law enforcement."

"What the fuck does that even mean?"

"That I have resources, people who owe me, and if I have to cash in a few favors for you, I'll do it in a heartbeat."

"You would?"

I palmed his cheek. "We're friends, man. I got your back. Come on. Let's make sure your car is drivable."

A section of the front passenger side had cracked and was hanging lower. "Shit! Look at this."

"It's okay. It looks like it's just one piece. What is that, fiberglass?"

"No, carbon fiber." Caden shook his head. "There's blood all over."

I stripped off my shirt and wiped most of the blood off. "There's a hose on the side of the aviation building. Spray it down before you go."

Caden frowned.

"It's going to be okay. Stop worrying and go home. I'll call you as soon as I know something."

"Can't I come with you?"

"I don't think that's a good idea. We have to keep this low profile."

Sitting in my family room, the phone buzzed. Again. It was Caden. I swiped away the fifth call he'd made in the hour since leaving the track. This had to be done in person. I grabbed my car keys and headed out.

Despite ringing the bell four times, Caden didn't answer. I dialed his number. "Beck, what happened?"

"You home?"

"Yeah, how's the—"

"I'm standing on your porch. Open the door."

"You're here? At my house?"

"Yes."

"Hang on."

The door cracked open. Caden stayed out of view. "Hurry in."

Caden's eyes were red. He slammed the door shut. "How is the kid doing?"

"Sit down."

"No! Tell me."

"He didn't make it."

"Don't play with me, man."

"I'm not. He died on the way to the hospital."

"Oh no. No, no, no! This can't be happening."

I threw up my hands. "Calm down!"

"But what am I going to do? I killed a boy."

"We can manage this."

"What about the cops? They're going to come after me. Maybe I should get a lawyer."

"Don't do anything. Especially don't get a lawyer involved."

"But how am I, I mean, what should I do? The parents are going—"

"Sit tight. I have a lot of connections. What I'm learning is the kid's parents are dead. He was living with an alcoholic uncle."

"I don't understand. What does that have to do with anything?"

"No one is looking for the kid. Okay? His friends left when we chased them away. He was the only one to come back."

"Beck, what the hell are you saying?"

"He never made it to the hospital. I know the guy who owns the ambulance company. Maybe we can work something out."

"Work what out?

"To keep all this between us."

Caden paced the room. "How can you do that?"

"People owe me a lot of favors."

"But a kid died."

"I know that, but keep in mind he lives in Immokalee and has no mother and father."

"The newspapers are going get ahold of this."

"Don't worry about the press. They're gigolos, hot on something until they move on to the next thing."

"What about the police? Once the body is found, they're going to trace it back to me. I should admit what happened."

"Nobody is finding any bodies."

He stopped pacing. "What do you mean?"

"I told you to let me handle it. It'll be like the kid ran away or somebody kidnapped him."

"But there was, like, ten people who saw it. Somebody is going to say something."

"Everyone that was there owes me, okay?"

He massaged his chest. "I can't breathe."

"Lie down. It's just a panic attack."

52

Sipping a second coffee, the burner I used with Mario buzzed. “Hey, where the hell were—”

A deep voice said, “We have your friend.”

“What?”

“Yesterday morning, we picked up your boy, Mario.”

“Who’s we?”

“You want to see him again, you need to talk to our boss.”

“Who is this?”

“Walmart parking lot. The one near Lely on Collier Boulevard.”

“I want to talk to Mario.”

They handed the phone off. “Beck.”

“Mario, are you okay?”

“Yeah. They grabbed me—”

“That’s enough. Be there at two today.”

“I’m not going anywhere until you tell me who you’re with.”

“Royal.”

The phone fell out of my hand. I picked it up. “Hello?”

They’d hung up.

Royal? He was alive? Where? How? I shook my head. Or was it his guys? Where was Mario being held, and were they looking to exchange him for me? I paced the room. If they wanted to kidnap me, why hadn't they done so? I was pretty sure no one had been following me. But the truth was, I'd let my guard down after Royal's boat exploded.

This was the payback for destroying Royal's alibi. I'd underestimated him. He was far more dangerous and cunning than I'd figured. If he'd faked his death, the cops had bought it because Royal owned the medical examiner who'd signed off that it was his body.

I had three hours. Larson might know something. He answered on the first ring. "Hey, Beck, the Peterson money just hit."

"They got Mario."

"Who?"

"They said it was Royal."

"Who said?"

I told him about the call. He said, "Damn, if Royal is alive, he's smarter than I figured."

"Have you heard anything?"

"Nothing more than that it's business as usual for them."

"This is crazy."

"It's got to be him. If you think about the whole boat thing, right before he's being sent away, it makes sense it was a scam."

"Where do you think he could be?"

"That's a tough one. You said they wanted to meet down in East Naples."

"Yeah."

"He can't be coming to you. That'd be too dangerous if you'd notified the authorities."

"They'll have scouts looking out, but I don't see him coming out of hiding either."

"Some years ago, he had dealings with the Miccosukee tribal leaders."

"He did? With what?"

"There were a couple of businesses—a gas station-convenience store, and an airboat operator just outside the reservation's borders. The Miccosukee wanted them out and needed to put distance between them doing it. So, they hired Royal to, uh, shall we say, persuade them."

"I'm surprised the tribe got involved with someone like Royal."

"Are you kidding me? They have an entire stable of homegrown enforcers who'd give Royal and his gang a run for their money."

"Can you make some calls? I need intel if I'm going to meet them."

"Sure."

"Thanks. Move it. I only have two hours."

"Of course. But you need to seriously consider whether meeting them is a smart move."

"They have Mario. I can't let him swing in the wind."

"They don't want him. They want you."

"Then why didn't they try and grab me?"

"Don't discount yourself. You've got a sixth sense. The easy thing to do was to use Mario to get to you."

"What do you think will happen if I refuse to go?"

"Hmm. Difficult to say, but they'd probably escalate."

"You don't think they'd hurt him or . . ."

"Royal likes to keep as low a profile as possible. Dead bodies bring attention. But if it's one of his guys running this, all bets are off. Most of those guys don't think an hour ahead."

"It has to be Royal. He orchestrated a fake death."

"It worked. I wouldn't want to the be the medical examiner who signed Royal's death certificate."

"Royal needs to be careful. If it comes out he's alive, it'll embarrass a lot of people. The Lee County Sheriff's Office will have to hunt him down with everything they have."

"It'll be messy. Just make sure you're not collateral damage, Beck."

"It's not the right word, but Royal is pragmatic."

Larson scoffed, "That's a first, calling a hardened criminal pragmatic. You're downplaying the danger. You want to go, go. But be honest about what you're stepping into."

"I am, don't worry. Just sniff around, and let me know if you find anything."

53

The smell of rain was in the air as I took the stairs to Caden's house and looked east. Dark clouds were rolling in off the Gulf of Mexico. I had to send a second text to get Caden to answer the door.

"What, were you sleeping?"

He shook his head.

I clicked a light switch, saying, "Put some lights on. This place is like a dungeon."

"Hold on! Someone's watching me."

"From where?"

"The back." He cracked the drapery. "He was right there, in a small boat."

"He's probably fishing."

"No. He was staring at my house."

"You're imaging things."

He released the curtain. "No, I'm not. He'll be back."

"You got to relax, Brett."

Caden dug in a kitchen drawer. He came up with a vial and put a spoonful of coke to his nose.

"What are you doing? It's only ten in the morning."

"I couldn't sleep, so I took an Ambien an hour ago. Now I gotta wake up."

"You start with those sleeping pills, you'll never get off them, and you need a shower."

He shrugged, snorting another hit. Pocketing the vial, Caden asked, "You said you had to tell me something. What is it?"

"We have a problem."

"What kind of problem?"

"Somebody who knows about the kid is getting cranky."

"Cranky? Fuck him. You know how I feel?"

"He's making noise."

"What the hell does that mean?"

"He's threatening to talk."

"Who? What motherfucker is it?"

"One of Stone's guys. He's looking for money."

"Fuck him."

"Don't discount it. It's something to consider."

"You said they owed you! And everything was all right."

"I'm doing the best I can. Don't forget; nobody ratted you out to the cops."

"I knew it was bullshit. I should've gone to the police. Now I'm going to look bad—"

"Hold on, we can contain this if we pay him."

"What is the bastard looking for?"

"He only wants a couple of hundred thousand."

"Only? That's a ton of money."

"It's a lot cheaper than hiring a lawyer to defend yourself in a murder case. A good defense lawyer is going to run you a thousand an hour, and they'll string it along. You'll go bankrupt before you go on trial."

"Murder?"

"What do you think? You not only killed him, but you took off. If you didn't run from the scene . . ."

"You told me to!"

"Look, we are where we are. Bottom line is this is a little problem that can be dealt with. You pay the man, and it goes away."

"How do I know he's not going to ask for more?"

"He won't."

"But how do I know?"

"If he does, I'll"—I made air quotes—"take care of him."

"What do you mean?"

"Some things are better left unsaid."

"What are you saying? That you'd have him killed?"

"Don't worry about me. You're the one with the problem. I'm just trying to help you navigate it."

"But I need to know."

"What you need to do is come up with four hundred thousand. In cash."

"You said a couple of hundred, and now it's four hundred?"

"Stop complaining. You know it's a bargain, especially when you consider you'd be tied up dealing with it for the next two years."

"No, that's crazy. I can't get that much cash in one shot."

"How much can you put together?"

"Fifty, maybe sixty grand in cash."

I shook my head. "That's not going to cut it."

"How much do I need to come up with?"

"All of it. Get fifty in cash, and I'll get you the bank info to wire the rest. It'll be a bank overseas that can't be traced."

Caden sighed. "Okay. All right. I need a couple of days to sell some stuff."

"Why don't you get rid of a car?"

"No way!"

"You have six cars."

He lowered his voice. "It's just five."

"Oh yeah, I forgot about the scam."

"And I'm not getting full value for it."

"Nobody needs that many cars."

"I love my wheels."

"Maybe you could sell one to me? I'm looking for a new one."

"No, I can't lose another one."

"Think about it."

"No, forget it."

I stood up. "All right, I'll text you the wire instructions."

"You're leaving already?"

"Yeah."

"Hang around. We can order something in."

"I got a ton of stuff to do today."

"Like what? Can't you just hang for a bit?"

"Don't tell anyone, but I've got a meeting with a big-time politician." I smiled. "He's way up there and I have him by the balls."

"How'd you do that?"

"I have to run."

"When are you coming back?"

"Hard to say. This bigwig is flying me to Orlando in a private jet."

54

A STEADY STREAM OF SHOPPERS WAS ROLLING CARTS IN AND out of Walmart. I parked in the center of the lot. Scanning the area, I saw it—a black Escalade with darkened windows.

It pulled alongside, and the front passenger window slid down. "Leave your phone behind and get in."

"Where are you taking me?"

"You'll find out. Get in."

I stuck my two phones in the console and got out. The back door of the Cadillac opened. I peered in. There were three of them. Two in the front and one in the back seat. They were huge.

More gold was hanging from their necks than was on display in Tiffany's. The car lurched forward. The hulk in the front seat turned around on his knees. "Get over here."

I nudged forward. The goon next to me pushed me closer. "Get your hands off me!"

"Shut up."

The two men patted me down. "He's clean."

The guy next to me handed me a black bag. "Put this over your head."

"What?"

He pulled up his T-shirt. A gun was tucked in his pants. "Put it on, or I'll do it for you."

The fabric scratched my face. "How long do I have to wear this crap?"

"Relax, Beck. We got a long ride ahead of us."

After ten minutes, my back was pressed into the seat. We were going up an incline. A long one. Then downhill. The only thing that made sense was a bridge. "We going to Marco?"

"Shut up."

The car made a series of turns. We slowed down and stopped. "We here?"

"No."

The car pulled forward and stopped. I heard a garage door opening. "Let me take this thing off." My hand was slapped away from the bag.

"I'll tell you when!" An arm reached across my chest, opening the door. "Get out."

Hearing the other doors open, I swung my legs out. A hand grabbed my forearm as I got out and adjusted to the heavy air. "This way. Watch your step."

A blast of cold air chilled the sweat running down my back. I was steered into a room, and the door closed behind me. I took off the bag. Dark drapes covered a slider.

"Where are we?"

"Sit down."

"Where's your boss?"

"We're out of here in ten."

"Where to?"

He shoved a bottle of water at me. "How many times I gotta tell you to shut the fuck up?"

I guzzled the water.

"Hurry up. Put the bag back on."

Two of them talked as they guided me outside. It sounded like we were walking on wood. Then the surface moved underfoot. It was a dock. "Step up."

They helped me onto a boat and shoved me into what I envisioned was a covered area. "Lay down and don't come out until I say."

The boat moved slowly at first, and then the front rose and we were moving under full power. Several hours later, we slowed to a crawl. One of them said to the other, "Jump off and tie us up."

We docked and I was led inside. The bag was pulled off my head. A bearded Royal was sitting in a corduroy recliner. His gold tooth gleamed as he smiled and said, "You need to take a pee?"

"No. What the hell am I doing here?"

"Sit down." He turned to his men. "Get him something to drink and go pick up a couple of pizzas. One with the works. And get some real Pepsi, none of that diet shit."

"Where is Mario?"

"He's with my guys."

"Where?"

"He's okay."

"Let him go. You have me now."

"We will. After we talk."

"How can I be sure he's okay?"

Royal grabbed a phone off the table and made a call. "Put him on. His daddy wants to talk to him."

Royal put the phone on speaker. "Hello?"

"Mario! It's Beck. Are you all right?"

"Yeah, I think Royal's guys got me. Where are you?"

"Hang in there. They said they're going to release you in a bit."

Royal disconnected the call and tossed the phone on the

table. He stared at me for a full thirty seconds before saying, "I know it was you."

"What are you talking about?"

Royal gave me a stony look you could rappel down. "You fucked with my alibi."

"You got that wrong."

"We go back, Beck. And we did some good business together. It insults me to have you deny it. It was you and your boy Mario. Admit it."

All I could think of was the scene in *The Godfather* where Michael Corleone was trying to get his brother-in-law to admit he'd set him up. Carlo caved—and was strangled to death minutes later.

"I don't know where you got your info, but it's wrong. Dead wrong."

"I thought you was smarter than that."

I wanted to stay alive. "Why'd you take me all the way to wherever the hell we are?"

"You're a freelancer, a kinda mercenary for hire. But there are some lines you ain't supposed to cross."

"I respect all my contacts."

Royal scoffed, "Even though it ain't my nature, I'm willing to let you off from selling me out."

I stayed silent as he tapped a Marlboro out of a pack. My craving for a smoke skyrocketed. He clicked a lighter and took a drag.

The smoke streamed out of Royal's nostrils. "You can even things out, and we stay friends."

"Friendship is good—"

He scowled. "Right now, we ain't friends. You're an enemy."

"Come on, Royal. You know—"

"I know what I know. You want me to cut your ass some slack? You gotta earn it."

"I didn't do anything, but tell me, what do you want?"

The cigarette's tip glowed red. Royal blew the smoke out and leaned forward. "You got contacts in the prosecutor's office."

"I wouldn't say—"

"Let me fucking talk!"

"Okay, go ahead."

"You want to save your ass and your buddy's, you gotta get something done."

"What?"

Royal reached for the pack of smokes. "Listen carefully."

55

"YOU CAN TAKE OFF THE BAG."

The Escalade stopped in the Walmart lot. "Get out."

I hopped out and slammed the door. The black Cadillac pulled away, and I jogged to my car. Pulling the door open, I grabbed my phone. There were seven missed calls from Caden. He'd have to wait. I dialed a number.

"Mario, they let you go?"

"Yeah. I'm on fucking Pine Island, waiting for an Uber."

"I'm down in Marco. You want—"

"Was this Royal's guys?"

"Yep, he's not dead."

"What?"

"I met him, somewhere. I think it might have been in the Keys or something."

"What the hell does he want?"

"Meet me at my place tonight, say around eight. I have to go see somebody now."

Sitting at one of the Coastal Kitchen's outdoor tables, my gaze bounced between the menu and the parking lot. Digging into the bread basket, there was no doubt I was getting the grouper sandwich. The question was whether the side was going to be sweet-potato fries or something healthier.

I raised a hand when O'Leary peeked into the tented area. I'd never seen him in shorts. I swiped away another call from Caden as O'Leary pulled a chair out. He asked, "Hey, what's so urgent?"

"Are you eating?"

"No, I ate already."

I signaled the waitress. "I'm starved. Hold on." I gave my order. O'Leary asked for a glass of chardonnay. The server left as my phone vibrated. It was Caden. Swiping it away, I leaned forward and lowered my voice. "Royal is alive."

"Nathan Royal?"

I nodded. "Yep, he faked his death to avoid going to prison."

"And how do you know this?"

"I met with him a couple of hours ago."

O'Leary put both hands on the table. "Hold on, now. Are you telling me you saw him? Where?"

"His guys picked me up in East Naples. They made me wear a hood, but I think we went to Marco and caught a boat to the Keys."

"And you have no doubt it was Nathan Royal?"

"A thousand percent."

O'Leary sat back. "He's got the Lee medical examiner on his payroll."

The server set down my food and O'Leary's wine. "Looks like it."

"Who the hell was the body on the boat?"

"Royal said it was an addict who'd OD'd." I shoved two fries into my mouth.

"Involuntarily, I'll bet."

"Could be."

"Could? How convenient, a guy his size OD's the day he runs."

I picked up my sandwich. "He could have had him cooling in a fridge somewhere."

"What does he want?"

With a mouthful of grouper, I said, "A deal."

"This guy has watermelons for balls. He takes off before sentencing, commits fraud faking his death, and he wants a deal?"

I rejected another call from Caden. "He wants all charges, pending and anything connected to it, dropped."

O' Leary raised his voice. "Sure, sure, why not?"

"He's got information that'll put most of the Petrov gang behind bars for a couple of decades."

"Talk about shaking hands with the devil. What kind of info?"

"He didn't reveal too much, but as you know, most of the fentanyl in Georgia and Florida is smuggled in by the Petrov brothers."

"Between the frigging Russians and Chinese . . ." He shook his head. "With all the overdoses, fentanyl is a hot button right now, but I can't promise you the state attorney is going to sign off on anything. Royal wants to plea it down some in exchange, we can probably do that."

"He told me it's all or nothing."

"He doesn't hold a good hand. He's the one on the run. He knows we'll catch up with him soon enough."

"I don't know. He said he's got enough money and was heading to an island without an extradition treaty with America."

"Wasn't his mother Haitian?"

"I think you're right."

"Haiti and the Dominican Republic, the other country on the island of Hispaniola, don't have treaties."

"And Barbados, Jamaica, Trinidad . . ."

"You did some research."

I took a bite of a fry. "When he disappeared, I wondered if he'd gone to an island."

"Our office did as well."

"You think you can do something for him?"

"You're an advocate now?"

"Never. But he knows it was Mario and me that torpedoed his alibi."

"And he threatened you?"

"Kidnapped Mario, used him as bait for me."

"Is he all right?"

"For the time being."

"What's that supposed to mean?"

"You know Royal is dangerous."

"Yeah, but that doesn't mean he gets to do whatever he feels like."

I shoved my empty plate to the middle of the table. "Of course, but you take down the Petrov brothers, and you'll not only choke the supply of the crap they push, but the press will shine on your office like the June sun in Florida."

"Publicity doesn't do a damn thing for me."

"I know, but the noise will help when budget time rolls around. They wouldn't have the nerve to challenge whatever your office asks for."

O' Leary drank the last of his chardonnay. "To say this is delicate is putting it mildly. We're going to need something concrete if this is going to go anywhere."

"I'll see what Royal can offer."

He stood. "I don't like this one bit."

"Me neither, but it's the worst of the bigger-fish approach; Royal is a shark, but the Petrovs are a school of killer orcas."

Waiting for the check, I texted Caden that I would swing by his house in twenty minutes.

The outside of Caden's house was lit like Yankee Stadium. A couple of beeps sounded, and the door opened.

Glassy-eyed, he said, "Where the fuck you been?"

"If I told you, you wouldn't believe it."

Caden slammed the door and re-alarmed the house. He shoved his phone in my face. "I got trouble, man. Big trouble."

"What's going on?"

He tapped his phone and held the screen so we both could see. It was a video of the racetrack. "Where'd you get this?"

"Somebody sent it to me."

"Who?"

"How the fuck should I know. You told me you had it handled."

"Calm down."

"Calm down? It's footage of the accident. It's fucking evidence. I never should've listened to you. I should've gone to the police. Now they know it was me."

"Take it easy. If the cops knew, they'd have been here already."

"It's only a matter of time."

"Nobody is looking into this."

"How can that be?"

"You see anything on the news?"

"No."

"Exactly. I told you the kid had no parents and, well, it's sad, but it is what it is."

He shook his phone. "Yeah, well what about this?"

"We got to find out who it was." I took my phone out. "Let me check with the guy who took the video. He's worked a lot with me, and I trust him with my life."

"But it's my life he's screwing with."

"Don't worry, I got this."

A horn honked. After jumping, Caden exhaled. "That's what you said before, and look where I am."

"Nothing has happened."

"What are you talking about? They are coming after me."

I touched his arm. "We're in this together. If and when a threat emerges, I'll deal with it."

"I'm worried sick, man."

"Send the video to me. I'll have my guys track down who sent it."

"How are you going to do that?"

"Every video has a digital fingerprint that can be traced."

"Really?"

"Sure, and we can backtrack from the number it was sent from."

"But only the police can do stuff like that. We can't go to them."

I threw up my hand. "I have contacts. We'll find out who the hell is screwing with us."

"What if it came from a burner phone?"

"Trust me, we'll find who sent it."

"How? You don't register them. They have no phone records."

"We can identify where it was activated, then we find the store that sold it. Nine out of ten have surveillance cameras. We have ways. We'll get him."

"How long is it going to take?"

"Not long. If it was a burner, it'll take more time."

"What if he reaches out? Asks for money or something?"

"That would be good."

"Good? I can't be paying another guy."

"If anyone contacts you, it'll make it easier to ID him. If you get something, let me know. Send me the video and the number it came from."

"Okay. I'll do it now." Caden tapped on his phone. "I forwarded it."

"Good. I'll see you later."

"You're leaving?"

"I'll be back. Why don't you jump in the shower?"

Caden ran a hand over the stubble on his face. "How long until you're back?"

"As soon as my guy tells me who it was. Clean up and get some sleep."

56

CADEN DISARMED THE ALARM AND CRACKED THE DOOR OPEN. I slipped in. He went to tap the pad, and I said, "You don't need to put it on. At least not with me here."

"Only takes a second." He armed the system and turned toward me.

"Your nose is bleeding."

He ran a finger under it. "Damn." He pulled a wad of blood-stained napkins out of his pocket and dabbed his nose. "What did you find out?"

"It was easier than I expected. We know who sent the video."

"Who was it?"

"Guy named Peter Abernathy."

Caden's eyes narrowed. "Abernathy? I don't know the name."

"He's a nobody."

"Some nobody; he wants a million dollars, or he'll send it to *WINK News*."

"We'll handle it."

"How? How the fuck we going to deal with this? He sends it to the news, I'll die behind bars."

"I got a guy."

"And what's he going to do? If he gets the video, this bastard probably has copies."

"My guy specializes in eliminating problems."

"Eliminating? What the hell does that mean?"

"Exactly what the word means."

Caden's eyes widened. "He'd kill him?"

I nodded.

Caden smiled. "When?"

"Best to move as fast as possible."

"Let's get it going."

"We need to meet up with my guy."

"In person? Can't you do it for me?"

"No, he's quirky that way. Insists on face-to-face things. He's old school. Doesn't want to leave a trace."

"That's good, that's good."

"He wants two hundred thousand."

Caden frowned. "I guess that's reasonable, given, you know . . ."

"You give me the money, or you can come with me and we deposit it right into his account."

"Go to a bank? Why do we have to do that?"

"He's superstitious, feels it's bad luck."

"This guy sounds strange."

"He gets the job done, but he's dangerous."

"He's not going to screw with me, is he?"

"He's the one doing the eliminating. We'd have it over him if he pulled anything."

"Yeah, right. What's his name?"

"I can't say. For now, let's call him Mr. X."

"What's the big secret?"

"He's super cautious. He wants to tell you, he will."

"Okay. We gotta get this done fast. That video gets out, I'm totally screwed."

"When do you want to go see him?"

"As soon as possible."

"I'll set it up. But you have to be aware, he operates from a place far away from here."

"That's good, right? Where is he?"

"It's good, but like I said, he's real cautious, and he doesn't let anybody know where he is."

"I like this guy."

"We'll be wearing hoods over our heads."

"Like a kidnapping?"

"Kind of. You cool with that?"

"I guess. I just want this dealt with. And as fast as possible."

A strong breeze was blowing. Dark clouds hung over Bayfront. I was the only diner sitting at an outside table at EJ's Cafe. I was halfway through a stack of their whole wheat pancakes when O'Leary walked into the covered area.

"Hey."

He pulled a chair out. "That's a lot of syrup, Beck."

"And it's damn good. You want a coffee?"

"I'm good."

I waved off the server and pushed my plate aside. "What did the boss say about a deal with Royal?"

"Before or after he questioned my sanity?"

"It was that bad?"

"Lukewarm is pushing it."

"All right. It's still alive, then."

"Life support is more like it. You're going to need to get me something big to change their minds. When I told them Royal was alive, the ass-covering went into full gear. Do you understand how this makes the department look?"

"It's tough, I know. But taking out a fentanyl gang . . ."

"And if he killed the homeless man, we can't look past a homicide."

"Let me see what I can find about that. Look, I want Royal to get a lethal dose of whatever prisons use these days, but we need to string him along, see what we can get out of him."

"Be careful what you promise him."

"I'm going to take another trip to see him."

"Be careful, Beck. I've got a bad feeling about this."

57

Caden got into my car. "I didn't know you wore glasses."

"I ripped my contact lens this morning."

"I don't know how you put those things in your eyes."

"You can get used to anything."

As we drove to the pickup point, Caden took out his vial of cocaine. I said, "If anything, you should be taking a relaxer, we got a long ride ahead of us."

"I'm okay."

"You know, this guy, he's also a dealer."

"He sells coke?"

"Yep, and harder stuff. Probably give you a good deal, if you buy enough."

"I need a new supplier. The prick I use has been cutting his with garbage."

"You got to be careful, a lot of dealers are lacing their stuff with fentanyl."

"What about your mystery man? His shit clean?"

"Yes. He doesn't mess with fentanyl. Too many overdoses, and that attracts attention, which he doesn't want."

"That's good. If I forget, remind me to ask him."

"Here we are."

"Walmart?"

"Leave your phone in the car. They don't allow you to take anything with you, and they're going to frisk you."

"I like this guy even more."

Three hours later, we were escorted into the same room where I'd met Royal before. Royal swept in. His beard was getting long. He studied Caden for a couple of seconds before motioning us to sit.

I said, "Before we start, I need to talk to you about what we discussed, in private."

Royal said, "Pluck, take this cracker into another room."

Caden's face dropped. I said, "It'll only be a minute."

They escorted Caden out, and I sat on the edge of my chair. "Look, as expected, there's pushback on a deal for you. It's not going to be easy."

"Easy? That's not my problem. You're the fixer—fix it!"

"They want something concrete on the Petrov gang."

"I ain't giving up my get-out-of-jail-free card."

"I'm not asking you to. Just give me information to prove that you're going to deliver."

"Let me think about it."

"The other thing is him." I pointed to the empty chair next to me. "You help with his problem, and everybody is going to be happy."

"What problem?"

"Peter Abernathy. This guy is threatening him, and I told him you could make him go away, for good."

He smiled. "You want me to knock off somebody, and that's gonna help with the boys in blue?"

"It's complicated, and they didn't tell me too much. Look,

I'll ask them for more on this, but for today, just tell Caden you'll do it."

Royal stared at me.

I added, "And I can get him to pony up a few bucks to help you settle in on your new life."

"How much?"

"Fifty K."

"Make it fifty up front and another fifty if we gotta do it."

"That's a deal."

"If you fuck with me, Beck, I'll kill Mario, your girl Laura, Larson, everybody you know."

"Come on, Royal. We're both transactional kind of people. We make a deal, both sides got to win or it falls apart. I'm—"

"Shut up, Beck. You screw with me, I'll make them bleed out in front of you before I gut your ass. You got that?"

"Loud and clear."

"Pluck, bring that cracker back."

Caden hurried to the seat next to me. "Everything all right?"

I nodded. "Tell him what you want him to do."

Caden whispered, "Didn't you tell him? You said you arranged it."

"He wants to hear it from you. Isn't that right?"

Royal said, "Spit it out. I ain't got all day."

"Uh, there's this guy Peter Abernathy; he's extorting money out of me. You see, he has a video and—"

"I don't need no details. What do you want done with this Abernathy?"

Caden looked at me, I nodded, and he said, "I want him eliminated."

"That's some fancy word. You want him killed?"

"Yes."

"Well, then, say it."

"I want you to kill Peter Abernathy, and I'm willing to pay your price to do it."

"In cash."

Caden looked at me, I nodded, and he said, "Okay."

"We got ourselves a deal."

"That's it. You'll do it?"

"Yeah."

"When? It needs to be done fast."

Royal scoffed, "Don't push your luck, sonny."

I stood. "I'll get the money to you. Can you get your men to bring us back?"

Hoods over our heads, we got into the back seat of an SUV. The driver took off and Caden leaned into me, whispering, "Holy shit, that guy is scary as hell."

"Yep."

"Who is he?"

"Keep quiet until we're back."

58

THE ALARM BEEPED AFTER I HIT THE BELL A SECOND TIME. Caden opened the door, and I slipped inside.

The lines in Caden's face had deepened since the Immokalee race.

"You still not sleeping?"

"No. I can't relax with all this shit hanging over my head."

I smiled. "You're going to sleep like a baby now."

"What? What's going on?"

"Mr. X took care of the problem."

"What? He got Abernathy?"

I shoved my phone in his face. The screen had a photo of a bloody corpse in the woods.

"Holy shit. This is crazy. I can't believe it."

"Believe it."

He stared at the image and smiled.

I reached for my phone. "I told you everything would be okay."

Caden hung his head. "I don't know how to thank you."

"No problem. I'm going to see our friend. You have the rest of the money?"

"Yeah, let me get it. Should I give him a tip or something?"

"No, keep it professional."

As Caden headed down a hallway, he said, "Man, this guy saved me. I can't believe it; it's over."

Caden came back with a duffel bag. "You want to count it?"

"Is it all there?"

"Yeah."

"If it's not, Mr. X is going to be pissed."

"No way I would screw with him."

"Smart man."

"After you pay him, I'm home free, right?"

"Absolutely. You won't have anything to worry about."

"What if something else comes up? Can Mr. X fix it?"

"If not him, I have plenty of other contacts."

"Man, am I glad I ran into you."

I extended my fist, and he bumped it, saying, "We got to celebrate. Let me take you out tonight. How does Delmar sound? I'll get us a nice table on the deck, or inside if it's too hot."

"Sounds good. What time?"

"Seven thirty."

"See you then."

I put the duffel bag on the passenger seat and pulled away. Waiting to make a turn onto Vanderbilt Drive, the burner cell in my pocket vibrated.

It was Pluck, Royal's right-hand man. "Hello?"

"He wants to see you. Tomorrow."

"Okay. What about?"

"Same pickup spot. Just you. Ten in the morning."

Click.

Was Royal ready to hand over information on the Petrov gang? Or had he rethought things?

Passing La Pescheria, Caden's voice could be heard over the milieu of diners. I skipped up Delmar's steps to the deck. Caden was talking through the open doors to someone seated at the bar. He had on a black-and-white-checkered shirt matching the patio's flooring.

Sitting next to him was a woman with lemon-yellow hair. Her white top was straining to contain her formidable breasts.

Caden saw me and smiled. "Here he is."

We shook hands. Grabbing the bottle of champagne in the ice bucket, he said, "Take a glass, we need to toast."

I said hello to his date, and Caden said, "Sylvia, this is Beck. You got a problem, he's your man."

I smiled.

Caden poured a glass of bubbly and handed it to me. "You gotta be careful, Syl, he knows a lot of badass people."

She wiggled in her chair. "You do? What kinda job you got?"

I sat down. "I work in finance."

Caden said, "Yeah, right."

Raising my glass, I kicked his shin under the table and said, "But I don't like to talk about work when I'm off. Here's to life."

We clinked glasses. Rifling through excuses to make my exit, Caden said, "Syl, this is the guy I was telling you about. He got me out of a jam, like that." He snapped his fingers. "It would've taken me a lot longer—"

I stood. "Brett, I need to talk to you about something, in private."

"Sure, man."

He followed me down the stairs to the sidewalk. I retreated

to the courtyard of the next building. Standing behind a metal sculpture, I said, "What did you tell your girlfriend?"

"She ain't my girlfriend. I just met her last night at Campiello's. You should've been there, man. We had—"

"You talk too much. I told you to keep your mouth shut."

"I didn't say nothing."

I lowered my voice. "You could blow it all. I don't care. It don't mean anything to me if you go to jail."

"Ah, come on, Beck. I didn't say—"

"Mr. X finds out—and he will—that you've been shooting your mouth off, you're going to wish you went to prison."

"I'm sorry, man. I didn't say much, just, you know, I was thanking you and stuff."

"I don't want my name mentioned or anything I do. You hear me?"

"Yeah, yeah, no worries."

"You say a word, it won't be pretty."

"My lips are sealed."

"Keep it that way. I'm out of here."

"Wait. You're not staying for dinner?"

"You ruined my appetite."

59

I STUCK THE PHONES IN THE GLOVE BOX OF MY CAR AND GOT into the black Escalade. Royal's right-hand man, Pluck, was in the passenger seat. Another henchman, Griff, sat next to me. He whipped a hood at me.

"How many times I got to wear this? I've been there several times already."

Pluck said, "Put it on."

I took my glasses off and slipped the bag over my head. "Wake me up when we get there."

There was no way I could nod off. Royal made me jittery. He was dangerous, and though somewhat predictable, he'd snapped a couple of times in the fifteen years I'd known him.

Was counting on the belief that he needed me a miscalculation? Royal had the money to escape to an island of his choice and live in luxury. But he'd lose power.

I was no head doctor, but I'd seen Royal wield fear like a maestro. He got a dopamine hit from doing it. It would be hard for him to leave that feeling behind.

Though he earned his money in an unconventional way, Royal shared a common trait with people who'd earned mega money: they kept working, not for the riches but for the strokes that power bestowed on their egos.

The boat trip was shorter than the others. I was helped off. The walk on the dock was longer than before. A screen door squeaked open. Pluck warned me, “Step up.”

The door closed behind me, and a hand pushed me forward. Another door opened. He said, “You can take it off.”

I pulled off the hood and put my glasses on.

Pluck said, “Sit down.”

Royal had changed locations. The plantation shutters were closed, but there was more light in this room. A case of Zephyrhills water sat on the floor.

“Can I have a water?”

“Go for it.”

I poked a hole in the plastic and pulled out a bottle. As I put it to my lips, Royal walked in.

“Hey.”

Royal nodded. He lowered himself into a chair. “Quicker ride, huh?”

“Yep, but I could do without being hooded.”

Legs splayed and hand on his crotch, Royal studied me. “How can I trust your ass after you sold me out?”

“How many times do I have to tell you? I didn’t sell you or anybody out.”

“You’re still sticking with that bullshit?”

“If I did that to anybody, my reputation would be shot. Nobody would work with me.”

“You better keep an eye on your boy Mario.”

“He’s like a brother to me. But if it means anything to you, this here, what I’m trying to do, he’s out of the loop. Completely.”

“You fuck me, Beck, and you’re a walking dead man. You hear me?”

"You have no worries."

"You, dead; your boy, Mario, dead; your girlfriend, Laura, dead—"

"Come on, Royal. I understand the stakes, man."

Someone knocked on the door. Royal said, "What? I'm in a meeting!"

Nino stuck his head in. "Sorry, man. You said to let you know about, you know what."

"Is it on?"

"Yeah, twelve thirty tomorrow."

"All right. Leave me be."

Nino disappeared, closing the door.

Royal licked his lips. "I want all charges dropped."

"Look, it's easier for them to give you a new identity."

He bolted upright. "Like witness protection shit?"

"You wouldn't be in a program, but you'd have a new passport and ID and could disappear anywhere without worrying you're going to be hunted down."

"I ain't going alone."

"You want to take a lady friend?"

"No. I can pick up a squeeze anywhere. I need my boy."

"Who are you talking about?"

"Pluck."

"Oh. I don't know, two new IDs . . . that's asking a lot."

"They want the fucking Petrovs or not?"

"Take it easy. I'm just trying to figure out a way to make everybody happy. What does he know about the Petrovs that you don't?"

"Pluck!"

The door swung open. "Yo, boss, whaddya need?"

"You gonna be at the Petrov drop tomorrow?"

Pluck tucked his chin and looked at me. Royal said, "It's okay."

"Yeah, I'm there, like, on them all. You need something?"

"No. That's all."

Pluck left.

"You see?"

"Okay, if he's that deep with them, he'll be helpful. I'll do what I can for him, but if they won't budge, I'll still get it for you, okay?"

He nodded.

"Good. Now, how are we going to get the Petrov brothers?"

"Easy fucking peasy."

"It has to be something concrete."

Royal leaned forward and spilled the beans.

60

The sun was high in the sky and the traffic thick. A tractor trailer wriggled out of the line of traffic, turning onto Metro Parkway. It was heading into the area of Fort Myers packed with distribution centers.

The driver put the directional signal on, making a left into the Fort Myers industrial complex. It drove along the access road, passing the multi-football-field-long UPS facility and a regional warehouse for Publix, and turned into a driveway servicing a FedEx depot and Sun Glow Spirits warehouse. The truck proceeded to the liquor distributor's building. A plane roared overhead as the driver backed up to one of its six bays.

He got out, opening the trailer's rear doors as a pair of FedEx vans pulled away from their warehouse. The driver eased the trailer the rest of the way into the bay and hopped out of the cab holding a clipboard and disappeared inside the building.

The FedEx vans converged on either side of the trailer. The doors to the vehicles burst open and a DEA SWAT team piled out. Guns drawn, the agents scurried up the stairs of the loading dock, announcing their presence.

Most of the people inside the warehouse froze, but Pluck dashed behind a forklift truck carrying a pallet of blue barrels.

The lead agent shouted, “Everybody on the ground!”

Lights flashing, six patrol cars from Lee and Collier Counties screeched to a stop. Cops piled out, flooding the facility.

Amid the reading of rights, handcuffs were slapped on and suspects put into the back seats of marked cars.

A stream of Russian was cut short by an agent: “Shut up!”

The DEA agent in command walked over to a forklift and told the man seated on it, “Set the barrels on the ground and get off.”

Wearing a tank top with a cross dangling from his earlobe, the driver said, “I didn’t do nothing. I just work here.”

After the cargo was on the ground, the agent instructed, “Cuff him. We’ll sort it out later.”

The drug enforcement officer knocked on the side of a blue barrel marked Organic Olive Oil - Product of Spain.

He motioned to another agent. “Pop the lid.”

The agent donned a mask as the others stepped back. The top of the barrel clattered to the ground. He peered in, shining his flashlight into it. “It appears to be all liquid.”

“Any signs of a false bottom.”

The officer sized up the container. “No.”

“Open another.”

He popped another one open. “It looks like oil. Hold on, there’s something on the bottom.”

“Be careful. Get him a pole grabber.”

He dipped a gloved finger into the liquid. “It smells like real olive oil.”

The agent put the device in and pulled up a shrink-wrapped package. Oil dripped off the plastic, splatting onto the floor. “It’s filled with pills.”

“Don’t open it. It’s probably fentanyl.”

61

Pulling off Hickory Boulevard, I parked. "Come on, boy." I scooped Toby off the seat and headed to the entrance of the Bonita Beach Dog Park. I waded through knee-deep water before setting Toby on solid ground.

Toby took off for a group of dogs frolicking in the surf. They had more fun at the beach than most people did.

I retreated under the shade of a scraggly tree. Losing sight of Toby, I stepped closer, catching a glimpse of Mario approaching.

He dropped his sandals. "What's with all the water? There's no other way in here?"

"Hurricane Ian screwed with it. It gets worse when the tide rolls in."

"They going to do anything? Can't they fill it in?"

"It's not a priority. They're still dealing with a lot of other damage."

"So, what did you hear on how it went?"

I backed up to the tree line. "Really good. Both Petrovs were there and Pluck."

"Oh man, I would've loved to see that."

"Me too. The Petrovs have less emotion than a rock, but by all accounts the Russians went on a tirade."

"Screw them. How many got arrested?"

"Nine, but the word is a couple of the warehouse workers seem to have had no idea what was going on. But get this, one of the Petrovs' top guys is talking. He said the drugs were shipped out of Mexico to Spain, disguised as tequila."

"What? Why Spain?"

"Rather than trying to run it over the border, they shipped it in legitimate shipments of tequila from Mexico to Spain. Once it got there, they would vacuum-pack it and submerge it in barrels of olive oil shipped into Charleston."

"Wow. I got to say, these guys went out of their way."

"The Petrovs are good at what they do. They kept the circle of knowledge small and went the extra mile to disguise it."

"I'll say. That's an elaborate plan if I ever saw one."

"Better than mine?"

Mario laughed. "What did O'Leary say? He must be happy to one-up the DEA."

"You got that right. According to him, the DEA had no clue it was going on, and if Royal hadn't told us, they never would've caught on if the Petrovs didn't screw up."

"It's not too hard to get ahead of the feds."

I shook my head as my burner vibrated. "It's Royal."

"With all this, he's got to be anxious."

"That's an understatement. He's pinged me four times since the raid. I told him I needed two days, but he's pushing like crazy for his end of the bargain."

"Let him sweat."

"If all goes well, I'll go see him tomorrow."

"Royal's going to be pissed his boy Pluck got picked up."

"He thinks I'm going to get him released."

"Can you do something?"

"Why would I burn a favor on a cretin like Pluck? He'll be behind bars for a long time, where he belongs."

I was pouring oat milk into my coffee when a voice on the TV said, "Just in. Breaking news. *WINK News* is live at the Collier County Sheriff's Office where Sheriff Remin is about to make a brief statement to the press."

I hurried to the family room to be in front of the TV. The sheriff stepped to the podium.

"Good evening. I'd like to report on an important development regarding a major supplier of the most powerful drug on the street, fentanyl. Earlier today, in a multi-agency operation, including the Collier County Sheriff's Office, we arrested several members of a drug smuggling gang. Acting on a tip from an informant, my office enlisted the aid of the Drug Enforcement Administration and the Lee County Sheriff's Office and coordinated a successful raid on a notorious group known as the Petrov brothers.

"The gang, headed by Grigor and Zory Petrov, is the largest drug supplier in the state of Florida, with tentacles reaching all the way into South Carolina. The suspects apprehended today were in the midst of receiving a large shipment of fentanyl at a warehouse in Fort Myers. Among those taken into custody were Grigor and Zory Petrov, the leaders of the smuggling operation, and several of their gang members. The investigation into this criminal enterprise is ongoing, and we'll release pertinent information at the appropriate time."

I fingered the scar behind my ear as the sheriff said, "I have time to take two questions."

The camera panned the roomful of reporters waving their

hands. Sheriff Remin pointed to a man in the front row. "Brian."

A bald man in a blue-checkered shirt shot to his feet. "Brian Gallagher, the *Naples Daily News*. Sheriff, congratulations on the success of the raid. Given the multiple agency forces involved in the operation, our readers would be interested to know what role your office played in it."

Had the question been planted by the sheriff's PR people?

Remin said, "We played a critical role in, first, uncovering the conspiracy to smuggle and distribute this deadly drug, then we provided the specifics on the when and where this particular shipment was being received."

"Did you know the Petrov Brothers themselves would be there?"

"I can't comment. Next question."

Remin pointed to someone in the front row. "Kate."

A slender woman in a white pantsuit stood. "Kate Wilson, *WINK News*. The fentanyl crisis is taking a toll across many communities in Southwest Florida, and throughout the nation. You've characterized the operation you took down as an important and consequential, shall we say, cog, in the importation and distribution of fentanyl. Do you believe you've significantly interrupted the flow and that this is a turning point in ending the crisis?"

"I wish I could say yes. The fact is we've won a significant battle, but the war is far from won. Thank you for coming today."

The only way to end the cycle was to either remove the money being made from it or to kill demand. Too many, including a depressing number of politicians and officials, had their hands out.

My burner vibrated. It was Royal.

62

WALMART MUST HAVE HAD A BIG SALE GOING ON. I PARKED IN the last row and opened the clamshell packaging for the phone I'd bought yesterday. The back of the phone came off easily. I stuck the SIM card in and activated the burner; neutral locations offered another layer of anonymity.

The black Escalade snaked its way to my car. I popped the burner and my cell phone in the glove compartment and got out.

A darkened front window of the Cadillac lowered. Nino said, "Get in."

I smiled. "We've got to stop meeting like this." He raised the window. I slid onto the rear seat. The thug sitting there handed me the hood.

"This is getting old. Why do I have to put this on?"

"Shut up and cover your head."

The fabric scraped my cheek. Who else had worn this?

"Move to the edge of the seat."

Two pairs of hands frisked me. "He's clean."

I sat back and the Cadillac sped away. Eyes closed, I kept my senses alert as we made our way to Royal. The car slowed, then bounced. Had we left the road? I stiffened. "Where are we going?"

"Shut up."

The threat that Royal's animal instincts would take over was real. Were we going to a place that'd be easy for them to dispose of me? The car came to a halt and the doors opened. I lifted the edge of the hood.

"Hey! Don't fuck with us."

We were by the water. We hadn't driven the incline that marked the bridge to Marco Island. Where were we?

Being led to what I was sure was a dock, released much of the tension in my shoulders.

A hand grabbed mine. "Step up."

We were boarding a boat. It looked like Royal hadn't changed his mind. For the moment. The boat took off, and a spray of water sprinkled my arm before I was put below deck.

After an hour and a half, the boat slowed and maneuvered into a slip. We'd arrived. The driver cut the engine. "Let's get moving."

I stood. The boat bobbed. A hand grabbed my wrist and led me forward. "Step up." My left foot hit the dock. Then my right. We walked into a house. The door closed and I took my hood off.

A suitcase stood next to a table. Cases of soda and water were stacked on the floor. I grabbed a water bottle.

Royal entered the room. He shut the door and took a seat.

As I sat, Royal beckoned me closer. I moved the folding chair next to him. He said, "You got it?"

I dug into my back pocket. "Yep. Here you go."

Royal took the passport. He flipped to the photo page. "Byron West?"

"I like the name."

Mouthing his new identity, he brought the book closer.

Royal ran his thumb over the hologram. He nodded and closed the passport. "Looks good."

"See, I told you I'd get it for you."

"You had no choice, Beck."

"I don't know about that."

"I fucking earned it, is what I did."

He was right. "True, man. It was exactly what they wanted, but still it wasn't easy getting them to agree. I had to call in every favor I had in storage."

"What about Pluck?"

"They wouldn't do anything for him. Especially with the Petrov connection."

"I'm hearing somebody's ratting."

"Me too. Looks like it's one of the Petrovs' guys, Dimitri."

"Fucking Russians deserve it."

"So, where are you heading?"

"Not sure. Maybe home."

"Chicago? You've been in Florida too long. You can't handle the cold anymore."

"I know, maybe Houston or New Orleans."

I stood, extending my hand. "Well, good luck."

Royal grabbed my hand, pulling me close. He looked me in the eye. "Be careful, cracker."

I smiled. "Always am. Always am."

He let my hand go. "Take him back."

The door swung open. Griff said, "Put your hood on."

I turned to Royal. "Come on, man. We're done, you got what you needed."

"He don't have to wear it no more. Where's Nino?"

"Out back."

"Go get his ass."

"Uh-huh."

"Go ahead, get outta here."

We boarded the boat. It was a forty-footer but far from new. The water was Caribbean colored. It pulled away from the dock into the no-wake zone. I scanned the shoreline. My gaze settled on a sign, Captain Craig's Plantation Key. Royal was hiding out in the Florida Keys.

Something caught my eye. I looked north, and a flotilla of boats was racing south. I squinted. Were they police boats?

One boat peeled off, heading in our direction.

Royal's man noticed them closing in. "What the fuck? The fuzz?"

I said, "What's the matter?"

Griff said, "Keep your mouth shut."

Over the drone of our boat's motor, a loudspeaker was broadcasting, "Bring your vessel to a stop! This is an order from the Collier County Sheriff's Office. Stop!"

Our driver slowed down. The cops closed in. An officer threw a white bumper over the side and their boat sidled up to ours.

Two officers raised their guns. "Hands up."

We put our hands in the air.

"Don't move. We're boarding your vessel."

63

I POURED MYSELF THREE FINGERS OF TITO'S. PEOPLE THOUGHT all vodkas tasted the same, but it was easy to tell the difference. I checked the time and clicked on the TV.

Another annoying commercial from a personal injury lawyer. Didn't they know these advertisements amounted to prodding people to consider a scam? Had Munoz been influenced by how the money lawyers bragged about winning?

The commercial ended, and the logo for *WINK News* filled the screen. I put my feet up and sipped my drink as the introduction to the news ended. Naturally, they led with threats of the possibility of stormy weather. Then a brief glimpse of the coverage they'd planned for the night, including why I was watching.

Sitting behind a desk, the anchor said, "We lead tonight's broadcast with something straight out of Hollywood. Our viewers may recall a story we covered regarding a boat explosion off Lovers Key's coastline."

The newscaster was replaced by a video of black smoke billowing from a vessel adrift in the Gulf of Mexico.

"The craft was owned by Nathan Royal, who was due to be

sentenced in the days after the explosion. A body, believed to be Mr. Royal's, was recovered from the wreckage. But the tragic story didn't end there.

"As seen in this video, taken in Monroe County yesterday afternoon, an arrest was made in Key Largo. The person taken into custody was none other than Nathan Royal. It appears Mr. Royal faked his death and had been hiding out in a home on the island of Key Largo.

"A passport containing Mr. Royal's photo but issued under the name of Byron West was seized. Monroe County officials believe Mr. Royal was poised to use this new identity to disappear for good.

"As if that wasn't enough, Lamar White, the attorney representing Mr. Royal, claims his client was acting as an agent for the Collier County Sheriff's Office. Here is Mr. White as he spoke with our Kate Wilson earlier today."

The lawyer was standing under the courthouse's portico. The reporter asked, "Mr. Royal faked his own death to avoid being sentenced to certain jail time. How do you plan to plead?"

"Mr. Royal was a de facto agent of the Collier County Sheriff's Office. He offered information, critical information, that was instrumental in the recent arrest of the Petrov brothers."

"If he was working with law enforcement agents, why was he in hiding?"

"My client entered into an agreement with Collier County prosecutors for them to drop the pending charges in exchange for information that led to the fentanyl raid. He put his life at risk to bring down a criminal enterprise. He should be celebrated and under their protection, not in a jail cell."

"What proof do you have of this agreement?"

"A passport with Mr. Royal's photo under the name of Byron West was seized during my client's arrest. Why would they give him a new identity if he wasn't under their protection?"

"Are you sure the passport was legitimate?"

"Absolutely. We look forward to exposing the shape-shifting ways of the government. Once we put sunlight on the double-dealing the government engaged in, we are confident the judge will drop the charges during Mr. Royal's arraignment."

"We'll be covering the hearing—"

"Let this be a warning to anyone seeking a deal with the authorities. Be forewarned, they cannot be trusted."

64

THE COURTROOM WAS PACKED WITH THE PRESS AND INTERESTED citizens. I slid into a pew and studied the people in the first row of the defense side.

None of Royal's men were there. Pluck was behind bars, but where were the rest of his men? Word had gotten out that Royal had ratted on the Petrovs.

I surveyed the people in the rest of the rows. No familiar faces.

A bailiff, carrying thirty pounds of excess weight, stood.

"Please rise. The Court of the Twelfth Judicial Circuit, Criminal Division, is now in session, the Honorable Michael Jacoby presiding."

Everyone got to their feet as a door opened. A bushy-headed man in a black robe lumbered to his seat. The judge eased himself into his chair and said, "Arraignments are public affairs, but given the interest the first case has generated, I've decided to go a step further. During these proceedings, I'll allow them to be recorded."

He put his reading glasses on and said, "Please call the case."

"Case number 343433BZ, State of Florida versus Nathan M. Royal."

"Is the defendant present?"

Royal and his attorney stood. "Yes, Your Honor."

The judge picked up a document. "The defendant is charged with fraud, violating the terms of his bail, and obstruction of justice. How do you plead?"

"Not guilty, Your Honor."

"All right, Mr. Royal. I hope you take these charges more seriously than the charges that led to your conviction on assault. A conviction for which you will be sentenced during another hearing."

Royal's attorney, White, stood. "Your Honor, we'd like you to consider our motion for dismissal of the charges."

"And your legal basis for a dismissal?"

"Did you read our brief?"

"Not yet. Summarize it for the court."

"Mr. Royal entered into an agreement with the prosecutor's office. This accord stipulated that my client would provide information in exchange for the dropping of all charges related to his flight and to suspend the sentencing on a prior assault conviction."

White picked something up off the defense's table. He held it up to the judge. "This is a passport issued to the name of Byron West. But the photo is of Nathan Royal. Providing my client with a new—"

Judge Jacoby whipped his reading glasses off his face. "One minute, Counselor." The judge looked at the prosecutor. "Mr. O'Leary, what is the state's response?"

He scrambled to his feet. "Your Honor, the state is grateful for the information Mr. Royal provided but objects to a complete dismissal."

"Did you promise to quash all charges against the defendant?"

"Yes, but we're about to file other charges, serious—"

"What is the status of those charges?"

"We're working on the filings. It should be any minute—"

Jacoby bounced the gavel on his desk. "Case dismissed. Call the next one."

Royal pumped his fist in the air and hugged his attorney. Pictures were being taken at a Hollywood red-carpet pace.

Royal was free. I slipped out of the courtroom before he could catch sight of me.

65

I GRABBED THE LAST PARKING SPOT. IT WAS TACO TUESDAY, and the reason North Naples Country Club was as busy as Easter week.

It was standing room only, but unless there was a stampede, nothing could ruin the day. How long did it take them to collect all the license plates they used as wallpaper?

Beer in hand, Mario was sitting at a high-top watching a golf match. I slid onto a chair across from him. "Hey, tell them to change the channel to *WINK News*."

"What's up?"

"Hurry up, it's almost six, and get me a Tito's on the rocks."

He walked to the bar. The bartender pointed a remote in my direction, and channel five began playing.

Mario set my drink down. "What happened that you want to see?"

I pointed to the TV as the introduction to *WINK News* was ending. The eatery was loud, but captions were rolling across the screen.

"Good evening, Southwest Florida. We begin our broadcast

with another piece of a dramatic and complicated story that brings home the saying that truth is stranger than fiction.

"The story, involving a man who faked his death, has taken yet another turn. Yesterday, Nathan Royal, the man police believed had perished in a boat explosion, was being arraigned at a Collier County courtroom. Mr. Royal pled not guilty at the arraignment, but it didn't end there.

"In an unexpected twist, Royal's lawyer explained that his client had made a deal with prosecutors to provide information in return for dropping the charges against him. The prosecutors acknowledged the agreement, and the judge dismissed the case. Mr. Royal was released from custody and left the courtroom.

"However, as you'll see here, his freedom didn't last long."

A video of Royal, hands cuffed behind his back and being led into the police station, filled the screen.

"Just a couple of hours later, Mr. Royal was rearrested at his Fort Myers home. The charges this time involved a conspiracy to murder. According to our police sources, Mr. Royal and another man, Brett Caden, were caught on film making a deal to kill someone for money. Mr. Caden, a resident of Naples, was arrested this morning."

Bug-eyed, Mario looked at me. I reached into the pockets of my cargo shorts and pulled out my spy-camera glasses.

Mario smiled. The newscaster continued, "If convicted, both men could be imprisoned for decades. We'll continue to bring you updates on this unusual story. Let's find out what weather is in store for us for the rest of the week."

I chugged the rest of my vodka and threw a fifty on the table. "Let's get out of here. We have work to do. We'll meet up at my house."

As we stepped into the sunshine and walked to our cars, Mario lit a cigarette. I said, "Give me one of those."

I took one out of the pack he held out. "Celebratory smoke?"

Nodding, I lit the cancer stick and took a deep drag. "I'll see you later." I took one more pull and snuffed it out in the outdoor ashtray.

66

Driving to Orlando was a pain but necessary. Route 4 was jammed with tourists going or coming from the area theme parks. Disney knew how to move people inside their parks; why didn't the powers that be consult with them on traffic?

After I passed the exit for Universal Studios, the road opened up. I got onto Route 192, snaking my way in the dark to an industrial park in Windsor Hills. The guard at the gate made a call, and I parked in the nearly empty lot of a warehouse.

I grabbed the leather satchel lying in the passenger footwell and went to the entrance. A silver sign hung over the door: Unique FX.

A minute after sending a text, the door opened. Headphones around his neck, Maddox Ross stuck his fist out. "You're looking good, Beck."

"Thanks. You too, Maddox."

I pointed to his T-shirt. "I didn't know you were into classical music. Is that what you're listening to?"

He nodded. "I was into grunge, but George Lucas turned me on to Puccini and Debussy when I was interning on *Jurassic Park*."

I followed him inside. "From Kurt Cobain to Frederic Chopin."

Maddox chuckled. "If Lucas was listening to bagpipes, I would've tried it. But the reality is, classical music helps the creative juices flow. I don't why, maybe it's the emotional aspect, but things seem to come easier."

"Don't mess with what works." I pointed to a green structure occupying a darkened corner. "What's that?"

"We're building something for Universal Studios. They're looking at a deal with Marvel to do an attraction using Thor and the Hulk."

"Oh, those are lightning bolts?"

"It's nowhere near finished, but if it's not clear, we're going to have to take another look at it."

"No, it looks good."

"How's Mr. Larson doing?"

"Ray's fine. He said to say hello."

"He's a good man. If it weren't for him, I would've never gone out on my own. He really believed in me."

Larson was as smart as they came. It wasn't just his belief in Maddox; he also knew that the experience Maddox would obtain working with the creator of *Star Wars* would lead to opportunities. That's why he invested some of the money he'd won in the personal injury lawsuit. "He's special."

"The best there is."

"You went to college with Larson's son, Tommy. Do you still see him?"

"Sure. We roomed together at Texas A&M, and when you're roommates, the friendship generally lasts a lifetime."

A roar came from the deep end of the warehouse. "What was that?"

"Columbia is exploring another sequel in the *Jumanji* franchise. It's a secret project, so keep it under wraps."

I followed him into one of the offices lining a wall. "Of course. Is it going well?"

"Oh yeah, the authenticity you get using AI to build replicas is frightening."

"You can't tell what's real anymore."

"So true. We used AI in your model as well."

"It was better than expected, but this whole AI thing is so lifelike, it's scary."

He closed the door behind me. "The era of deepfakes is upon us, Beck."

I handed him the bag containing a hundred thousand in cash. "We really appreciate your help."

"Anytime. As long as it stays between us and I got the bandwidth to handle it, I'll help out."

"You want to grab some dinner?"

"Sure. I know a good Italian place with a wine list full of Barolos ready to drink."

67

Toby was waiting at the door. He was excited to see Mario. Dogs never forget someone, just like humans.

I headed into the family room. "You can play later, Toby. We have work to do."

"Come with us, boy."

Standing by the couch, I said, "Grab the other end."

We picked it up and moved it back. "That's good; it's off the rug."

"Let's move the cocktail table by the TV."

We set the table down. I got on my knees and rolled the area rug up. "Get the thin screwdriver in the drawer next to the fridge."

Mario handed me the tool. I carefully lifted a section of the wooden flooring, revealing the safe I'd had sunk into the foundation.

"Did it get wet from Ian?"

I put my fingers on the print reader. "No, it has a waterproof seal."

The safe flashed red, and the lock released. I reached in,

grabbing a duffel bag. Pulling the zipper open revealed wrapped stacks of hundred-dollar bills. "Put it on the couch."

The safe door clicked. I put my fingers on the pad, and it locked. I rolled the carpet back in place and checked that it lined up with the UV lines the sun had created. I said, "All right, let's put the furniture back."

We unloaded the bag, lining up the money on the counter. I grabbed a box of brown paper lunch bags.

Mario said, "How'd it go in Orlando?"

Stuffing a dozen packs into a bag, I said, "Except for the drive and the fact Maddox likes to drink expensive wine, it was good."

"How much was dinner this time?"

"A thousand. But it was a bargain. You should've seen the dummy the FX guys made up. It looked like a real kid. The blood was the right color and consistency. It was eerie."

"Believe me, I'm pissed I missed it."

"Royal got what he had coming to him."

"Amen. You never told me how they knew where Royal was hiding."

"I put a GPS locater in the heel of my shoe."

"Sweet. How much for Stone, O'Reilly, and their guys?"

"They wanted thirty K. I say we give them forty each."

"Well worth it. They should be working in Hollywood."

I took a band off one of the stacks, dividing it in half. "The ambulance thing cost us fifteen thousand."

"Larson getting his usual?"

"Yes. He called this morning. Puzo surrendered his law license."

"He can't do any more harm."

"We should give Larson something for using his Ferrari."

"Sure."

"I never thought I'd like it, but I'm going to miss driving his

Ferrari." I lifted the partial stack. "I'll give him the other half of this."

"That's fair."

As I stuck eight bundles into Larson's bag, Mario laughed. "What are you giving Abernathy?"

"Since I created him, I'll hold on to his fee."

Mario said, "The two most important pieces of this, the boy and Abernathy, didn't exist."

"Maybe, but they were renting space in Caden's head."

"They sure were."

"I want to give Peterson back two hundred of the three he paid us."

"That's a lot."

"It's the right thing to do. We still clear four hundred. We'll take a hundred and fifty each and keep a hundred on the side."

"Sounds good. What do you have lined up next? Anything juicy?"

"Ventura has something, but I don't know if it's right for us."

"What is it?"

"It involves a couple of heavy-handed people at child services."

"Sounds interesting."

"And depressing. I don't have all the details, but it seems a father went to jail and lost custody for abuse that may not have occurred."

"Hmm. Man, if it's true, it'd be something to fix."

"Yeah, but it might be too close to home."

"The parents have money?"

"I didn't get into it with Ventura."

"We should give it some thought."

"That's what I plan to do. But first, I need a couple of weeks off."

"Are you going anywhere?"

"Not sure."

"Why don't you try and get back with Laura?"

He knew me too well. "We'll see. Let's get this money dropped off."

THERE IS MORE TO COME IN THE ART OF PAYBACK SERIES.

STAY UP TO DATE!

FOLLOW DAN PETROSINI AT WWW.AMAZON.COM/AUTHOR/DANPETROSINI

While you wait for the next book in this series have you read, The Luca Mysteries?

Am I the Killer? - A Luca Mystery Crime Thriller: Book #1

ENJOY ANOTHER THRILLING SERIES.

START READING BOOK ONE OF SUSPENSEFUL SECRETS, **CORY'S DILEMMA.**

His big music career break . . . was because of a lie.

I hope you enjoyed reading ***Race To Revenge*** as much as I enjoyed writing it. If you did, I'd appreciate it if you would write a quick review on Amazon or your favorite book site. Reviews are an author's best friend and even a quick line or two is helpful. Thanks, Dan

The Luca Mystery Series

Am I the Killer

Vanished

The Serenity Murder

Third Chances

A Cold, Hard Case

Cop or Killer?

Silencing Salter

A Killer Missteps

Uncertain Stakes

The Grandpa Killer

Dangerous Revenge

Where Are They

Buried at the Lake

The Preserve Killer

No One is Safe

Murder, Money and Mayhem

Suspenseful Secrets

Cory's Dilemma

Cory's Flight

Cory's Shift

Art Of Payback

Race To Revenge

Other works by Dan Petrosini

The Final Enemy

Complicit Witness

Push Back

Ambition Cliff

You can keep abreast of my writing and have access to books that are free of discounting by joining my newsletter. It normally is out once a month and also contains notes on self- esteem, motivational pieces and wine articles.

It's free. See bottom of my website: www.danpetrosini.com

ABOUT THE AUTHOR

Dan is a USA Today and Amazon best-selling author who wrote his first story at the age of ten and enjoys telling a story or joke.

Dan gets his story ideas by exploring the question; What if?

In almost every situation he finds himself in, Dan explores what if this or that happened? What if this person died or did something unusual or illegal?

Dan's non-stop mind spin provides him with plenty of material to weave into interesting stories.

A fan of books and films that have twists and are difficult to predict, Dan crafts his stories to prevent readers from guessing correctly. He writes every day, forcing the words out when necessary and has written over twenty-five novels to date.

It's not a matter of wanting to write, Dan simply has to.

Dan passionately believes people can realize their dreams if they focus and act, and he encourages just that.

His favorite saying is – "The price of discipline is always less than the cost of regret"

Dan reminds people to get the negativity out of their lives. He believes it is contagious and advises people to steer clear of negative people. He knows having a true, positive mind set makes it feel like life is rigged in your favor. When he gets off base, he tells himself, 'You can't have a good day with a bad attitude.'

Married with two daughters and a needy Maltese, Dan lives in Southwest Florida. A New York native, Dan has taught at local colleges, writes novels, and plays tenor saxophone in several jazz bands. He also drinks way too much wine and never, ever takes himself too seriously.

He puts out a twice-a-month newsletter featuring articles, his writing and special deals and steals.

Sign up at www.danpetrosini.com

Made in the USA
Columbia, SC
23 December 2023

28452543R00187